Nose to the ground

The vizsla took off parallel to the creek, following a barely there path through the underbrush. After pausing to regain the scent, she headed off again with Meadow at her heels.

With a jerk on her leash, Grace pulled toward the creek, then stopped, looking up and down the bank. No scent.

Whoever they'd been trailing had crossed about two hundred yards up from the bridge, where the underbrush was thick. Were they friend or foe?

Meadow led Grace through the water and toward a thick stand of brush. She headed into the deepening shadows and paused to scan the sky. The clouds were thickening and—

Something rustled in the trees behind her.

A hand clamped over her mouth.

* * *

Mountain Country K-9 Unit

Jodie Bailey writes novels about freedom and the heroes who fight for it. Her novel *Crossfire* won a 2015 RT Reviewers' Choice Best Book Award. She is convinced a camping trip to the beach with her family, a good cup of coffee and a great book can cure all ills. Jodie lives in North Carolina with her husband, her daughter and two dogs.

Books by Jodie Bailey

Love Inspired Suspense

Mistaken Twin
Hidden Twin
Canyon Standoff
"Missing in the Wilderness"
Fatal Identity
Under Surveillance
Captured at Christmas
Witness in Peril
Blown Cover
Deadly Vengeance
Undercover Colorado Conspiracy
Hidden in the Canyon

Rocky Mountain K-9 Unit

Defending from Danger

Pacific Northwest K-9 Unit

Olympic Mountain Pursuit

Mountain Country K-9 Unit

Montana Abduction Rescue

Visit the Author Profile page at LoveInspired.com for more titles.

Montana Abduction Rescue

JODIE BAILEY

LOVE INSPIRED SUSPENSE
INSPIRATIONAL ROMANCE

Special thanks and acknowledgment are given to Jodie Bailey for her contribution to the Mountain Country K-9 Unit miniseries.

LOVE INSPIRED® SUSPENSE
INSPIRATIONAL ROMANCE

ISBN-13: 978-1-335-98001-4

Recycling programs
for this product may
not exist in your area.

Montana Abduction Rescue

Copyright © 2024 by Harlequin Enterprises ULC

For questions and comments about the quality of this book, please contact us at CustomerService@Harlequin.com.

® is a trademark of Harlequin Enterprises ULC.

Love Inspired
22 Adelaide St. West, 41st Floor
Toronto, Ontario M5H 4E3, Canada
www.LoveInspired.com

Printed in U.S.A.

Thine eyes did see my substance,
yet being unperfect; and in thy book all my members
were written, which in continuance were fashioned,
when as yet there was none of them.
—*Psalm* 139:16

ONE

He should have known this was a trap.

Ian Carpenter sped down a winding back road near Glacier National Park, pushing his old reliable pickup to the limits of its capabilities as he raced to save himself from his pursuers.

What was happening? The threat to his life had ended three months earlier when Ronnie Thornton died in prison, the last member of a crime family whose threats had driven Ian to take refuge in witness protection. It should have been safe for him to return to his hometown.

It wasn't.

Behind him, a sleek sedan kept pace, toying with him. The driver raced up on his bumper then backed off before charging again. Likely, he was searching for the right place to clip Ian's pickup and spin him off the mountain.

He had to get off the road and to good cover before that happened or they barreled into a populated area and put others at risk. Glacierville, Montana, rested peacefully in the valley, and the last thing he wanted was to see an innocent family caught up in this wild chase, the victims of whoever was running him down.

Gripping the steering wheel, Ian took a curve at a speed that made his palms sweat. Only his prior training with the

Peak County Sheriff's Department kept the truck from hurtling off the mountain.

His pursuer misjudged the curve. The back end of the car slipped to the outside.

Ian didn't slow to watch. He pressed the gas pedal to the floor, trying to reach the one place where he might be safe and help could potentially find him.

There.

The turnoff snuck up on him, and he wrenched the wheel, tearing through brush and past trees onto an old logging road that wound deep into the woods. He winced as branches screeched along the paint of his restored Ford pickup. When he'd first gone into hiding, the vehicle had been his outlet, the physical labor of repairs a way to block his fears and regrets from drowning him.

Best not to worry about a paint job when his life was on the line.

A large metal gate appeared in the center of the road. Ian slammed on the brakes and fishtailed to a stop just short of the barrier.

This was new.

Guess he was on foot from here.

Grabbing his pistol from a custom pocket on the side of the seat, he shoved the door open and raced into the underbrush. Ian barreled down the rocky hillside toward the densest part of the forest, where a creek cut a ditch at the base of Calham Mountain, about seven miles outside of Glacierville.

When he reached thick underbrush and deep shadows, he pulled his phone from his pocket and surveyed the area, trying to orient himself.

From the logging road above, the sound of gravel under braking tires skittered across his nerves.

He'd gained a lead, but not much.

Heart racing, he opened a new text then typed the number he'd long ago committed to memory. There was no one else who could get him out of whatever this was. 911. At our old place. Outsider

Typing out his old code name nearly knocked him back two years, but any emotion was drowned by adrenaline and urgency.

He sent the text along with a prayer that Meadow Ames would see it and come immediately.

Not that God had time for his prayers, but it was worth a try.

When he'd been undercover with a multiagency human-trafficking task force led by the US Marshals, Meadow had been his handler. If he ever needed her to back him up, it was now.

Otherwise, he was as good as dead.

Pocketing the phone, he listened. Judging from what sounded like wild elephants crashing through the brush above, there were at least two people in pursuit.

Who were they? This had to be about something other than the undercover op that had taken down the Thornton family's human-trafficking ring. Ronnie, the patriarch, had died awaiting trial in prison three months earlier. His son and their most trusted bodyguard had been killed in an explosion during a takedown gone wrong on the day Ronnie was arrested.

After Ronnie had hired an assassin who'd almost succeeded, Ian had been moved into witness protection, where he'd spent the better part of eighteen months in Texas living as Zeke Donner. With Ronnie dead, he'd been cleared to return to the area, though he'd been hesitant to do so.

Only his cousin's call for help had dragged him back.

Either some unknown foe wanted him dead, or he'd stumbled onto a greater mystery.

Well, he wasn't waiting to find out. Carefully, he crept toward the stream and the footbridge above it. He'd met Meadow there often when he had intel to pass along on the op. He would conceal himself in the underbrush to wait for her and any backup she brought with her.

Hopefully, she'd muster an army.

At the edge of the clearing, Ian stopped and scanned for a good place to hunker down. It would have to be far enough from the water to keep his pursuers from stumbling upon him but close enough for Ian to see Meadow when she arrived. He kept moving, careful not to break branches or disturb leaves.

Behind him and to the left, the sound of movement stopped.

Ian froze. Their stillness would make it easier for anyone listening to hear his movement.

"Hey, Deputy!" The shout rang through the evergreens and echoed off the slope.

Ian's breath caught in his throat. They knew he'd been a Peak County sheriff's deputy.

This wasn't some random act.

He shrank into the underbrush, hardly daring to breathe until his pursuers moved. They were only a few hundred yards away and would easily spot him if he tried to maneuver while they were hunting.

"You aren't getting away from us, traitor!"

Traitor?

Wait. That voice. It was familiar.

Sweat sheened his skin. It couldn't be. Silas Thornton was dead. DNA had identified his body in the rubble of a warehouse after a catastrophic explosion. There was no way he was stalking Ian through the Montana wilds.

Ian inched to the right, angling to see up the slope. Several hundred yards uphill, a woman crossed a narrow clearing, moving parallel to Ian's position.

Recognition jolted through him. Desiree "Des" Phelps had been Ronnie and Silas's chief muscle and their most trusted enforcer. Although built like a ballet dancer, she had the strength of a lion. A seriously angry lion.

Realization burned hot in his veins. They'd been played. After the task force had arrested Ronnie and rounded up his underlings, they'd surrounded a warehouse in Missoula to apprehend Silas and Des. The team tossed several flashbangs into the building, and one had ignited a fuel tank. Two bodies inside were incinerated, but DNA from two teeth and a toe had identified them as Des and Silas.

Clearly, the pair had sacrificed their own body parts in order to avoid prison, and now they were hot on his trail.

As they began to stalk the underbrush again, Ian eased along as well, keeping to the thick vegetation along the creek as he moved away from them.

An animal startled in the bushes nearby, racing up the slope.

A gunshot cracked through the trees, and three more followed, slicing through the air only feet from his position and sending panic through his system at the remembered piercing of a bullet that had nearly ended his life.

This was it. He was done.

Defenseless.

Paralyzed by fear.

Closing his eyes, Ian waited for death.

"This was a colossal waste of time." Deputy US Marshal Meadow Ames sat back in her chair and reached over her head, trying to stretch the tension from her shoulders. She'd been holed up in a conference room at the Glacierville, Montana, police department all day, hunched over computer files and physical files, studying the murder of Henry Mulder until her neck ached and her eyes burned.

Across the table, Elk Valley, Wyoming, police officer Rocco Manelli dragged his hands down his face. He looked as exhausted as Meadow felt. Like Meadow, Rocky was a member of the Mountain Country K-9 Unit, composed of law enforcement officials from across several Rocky Mountain states. "I've chased suspects for miles on foot and not been this exhausted." At his feet, his K-9 partner, a chocolate Lab who specialized in accelerant detection, yawned. Rocco grinned. "Even Cocoa has had enough."

"At least Cocoa is awake." At Meadow's feet, her partner, a vizsla trained in tracking and search and rescue, snored lightly. "Grace zonked out an hour ago." People often mistook Grace for a Weimaraner, although that breed was typically gray while her K-9 partner had a gorgeous rusty coat.

Shutting the laptop the Glacierville PD had provided so they could access the department's electronic files, Rocco gave her a rueful look. "I'm with you. This was a bust."

They'd spent the day digging through evidence and interviews in the homicide case of Henry Mulder, who'd been killed a few months prior by a serial murderer dubbed the Rocky Mountain Killer that Meadow and Rocco's interagency K-9 unit was hunting.

Ten years earlier, the killer's first three victims were found in a barn in Rocco's hometown of Elk Valley, Wyoming, on Valentine's Day. All were in their late teens and early twenties, and all were shot in the chest. They were graduates of Elk Valley High School and members of the now disbanded Young Ranchers Club.

A decade later, the killer was active again. Five months earlier, Henry Mulder had been killed in Glacierville, while

Peter Windham had been murdered in Colorado. More recently, Luke Randall had been killed in Idaho. Like the first three victims, they were each shot in the chest and found in a barn. They, too, were EVHS grads and former YRC members.

There was a chilling difference in the latest three killings, however. Stabbed into the new victims was the same typed note: *They got what they deserved. More to come across the Rockies. And I'm saving the best for last.*

In response to the murders, FBI Supervisory Special Agent Chase Rawlston had been tasked with heading the Mountain Country K-9 Unit. Fifteen K-9 officers from various federal, state and local agencies were working together to hunt down the killer before he could strike again.

Combing through the files in Glacierville had led to nothing but a literal pain in Meadow's neck. Neither she nor Rocco had taken a break since lunch, when they'd dashed to a café up the street for sandwiches then out to their SUVs to feed the K-9s and to check their phones, which the police department didn't allow inside rooms with evidence after a leak of confidential information several years before. Meadow longed for sunlight and a muscle-stretching run, even though the July weather was unusually warm.

They retrieved their weapons from locked storage, turned in the borrowed laptops and files, then headed into late-afternoon sunlight.

Rocco slid sunglasses onto his face. "You headed to your house?"

While the MCKU was investigating, home base was the Elk Valley Chateau Hotel in Elk Valley, where the first murders had occurred. That HQ was almost fourteen hours away, so they'd been authorized to stay in Glacierville while they dug into the Mulder homicide.

Because Meadow's home was only about thirty minutes from Glacierville, on the road to Missoula, she'd opened it up to members of the unit who were in the area, setting up a space in the guest room for the team members and their K-9 partners. "I am. You heading that way or going somewhere else first?"

Rocco glanced at his watch and then at the sky, where dark clouds were piling up on the western horizon. "I think I'll drive around and admire the scenery, mull over what we read today and what we saw at the crime scene yesterday. Give me a chance to clear my head. Might stop and eat at the farm-to-table place you told me about. All you ever have when somebody bunks at your house is cereal."

"You're the only one on the team who complains, food snob, but I understand wanting to take in the scenery. Just keep an eye on the weather." The mountains around Glacier National Park offered the kind of spectacular views that helped clear her head after a long day of dealing with murder and mayhem. It was one of the reasons she'd accepted the position with the US Marshals office in Missoula, where she'd been based before taking the temporary assignment with the MCKU. "I'll likely be asleep by the time you show up, but you know where the key's hidden. We've got to be up and rolling early since Chase wants a seven a.m. video conference with us all."

"Yes, Mom." Rocco headed for his SUV with Cocoa at his heels. "See you later."

Meadow clicked the button to open the rear of her vehicle, where Grace's custom kennel was located. The SUV had been outfitted with everything from a built-in water bowl to automatic windows and an alarm should the air-conditioning ever shut off while Grace was inside.

The K-9 bounded into the vehicle and settled in as Meadow filled the water bowl then shut the door.

Rocco was backing out when Meadow climbed into her vehicle. She grabbed her cell phone from the locked glove box and glanced at the screen.

The temperature warning flashed angry red.

Great. Meadow slipped the phone into its holder, positioned in front of an air vent, and cranked the AC. While it didn't often crack ninety degrees in Glacierville, the day had been unusually warm, and her car had been closed up for longer than normal. She rolled out of town and headed for home, waiting for the phone to cool down and power up.

She peeked at Grace in the rearview then pointed the car south. "You ready for one more night at home?" They'd wrap up odds and ends tomorrow and head back to Elk Valley the next day. It might be a while before she saw home again. The one plant she'd managed to keep alive had given up hope, but she'd watered it the night before and would water it again tonight. It had come back from worse neglect. "So, home, girl?"

Grace tilted her head as though she understood, then found a chew toy and busied herself with it. Grace's training had taught her that inside the vehicle was an off-duty space. Vizslas were known for chewing, and Grace was a champion at destruction if she didn't have something to keep her busy.

Meadow's shoulders had just begun to relax when her phone lit up and pinged repeatedly. She pulled into the parking lot of a coffee shop and popped the device free, flicking the screen to see if she'd missed many calls and emails. She doubted it, given that the team knew to call the police department if an emergency came up while their cell phones were out of reach.

She grimaced at the number of notifications. In the distance, the dark clouds continued to build. If she wanted to beat the coming storm, she'd need to get moving. "I'll try to make this quick, Grace."

The K-9 didn't seem to care. She and her chew toy were perfectly content.

Meadow opened the texts first, since the most urgent messages would be there.

Her fingers froze. Three notifications down was a number she didn't recognize, though the sender was clear.

Outsider.

She'd never expected to see that code name again. It swirled hot and cold around her heart.

Forget the rest of her messages, Ian's 911 took precedence. She slammed the phone into its cradle, jammed the SUV into Drive and roared out of the parking lot, headed for the mountains between Glacierville and Cattle Bend. Ian wanted to meet in their "old place," where they'd exchanged intel when he was undercover. That meant he was twenty minutes away, in Calham Nature Preserve.

She prayed the entire drive. There was no way to know what the threat was or how long Ian had been in the area.

She gripped the wheel tighter, ignoring the burn behind her heart. There was also no way to know why Ian hadn't reached out when Ronnie Thornton had died and the threat to Ian's life had ended.

He'd remained distant and silent while Meadow had pieced together the heart Ian could never know he'd broken. Despite the fact that he'd repeatedly talked about his aversion to dating and marriage, she'd managed to fall hard for the law enforcement officer with the light brown hair and deep blue eyes. There was something broken about him, something that her own heart had connected with. In the end, she'd wound up shattered when he went into WITSEC, and that pain was only magnified when the threat to his life ended and he didn't reach out.

Until now...when he needed help.

She roared into the parking lot at the trailhead, unsure if she was relieved or disturbed to see no other vehicles. At the rear of the SUV, she pulled her badge over her head and shoved it into her pocket, then removed the MCKU patches from Grace's harness. She had no idea what she was getting into, and sometimes it was safer not to be immediately identified as law enforcement.

She slung a small backpack over her shoulders, checked her sidearm, then plunged down the path toward the creek, where they used to meet when Ian was undercover and she was his handler. It was the one place he'd felt truly safe when they were working together on the human-trafficking task force, the one place they'd felt free to openly talk about everything from the case to their personal lives.

Where they'd become friends.

And where her feelings had grown deeper as time passed, while his had stayed firmly in friend territory.

Right now was the wrong time to be leading with her heart. Besides, she'd put her feelings for Ian on ice when he'd disappeared into WITSEC.

As Meadow neared the creek, she stepped off the trail to follow a narrow footpath that disappeared beneath the bridge.

No one was near.

Motioning for Grace to sit, Meadow listened, wary of calling Ian's name. Without knowing the nature of the threat, her options were limited. Calling out could put them in jeopardy.

If she had something of Ian's for Grace to sniff, she could set her partner onto his trail. Unfortunately, all she had was memories.

Thunder rumbled in the distance, and wind tangled the treetops.

She clucked to Grace, who trotted beside her as she inspected the clearing. Up the hill, someone had clearly walked through the underbrush.

Ian? Or someone else?

She carefully followed the trail, eyeing the ground and the bushes until…

A cell phone.

It felt as though her heart stopped for several beats as she knelt and inspected the phone, then flipped it over. It must have fallen from a pocket, landing on its corner. The screen was shattered, and the device appeared unusable. It either belonged to Ian, or to whoever had threatened him.

She'd take her chances.

She collected the phone, let Grace scent it, then gave her partner a moment to pick up a trail.

Nose to the ground, Grace sniffed in a small circle, then took off parallel to the creek, following a barely there path through the underbrush. After pausing to regain the scent, she headed off again with Meadow at her heels.

With a jerk on her leash, Grace pulled toward the creek then stopped, looking up and down the bank. No scent.

Whoever they'd been trailing had crossed about two hundred yards up from the bridge, where the underbrush was thick. Where were they heading now? Were they friend or foe?

She led Grace through the water and toward a thick stand of brush about halfway up the hill.

She headed into the deepening shadows and paused to scan the sky. The clouds were thickening and—

Something rustled in the trees behind her.

A hand clamped over her mouth.

TWO

Ian grunted as Meadow's elbow drove back into his ribs.

She spun, gun in hand, and aimed at his center mass before he could process what had happened. Beside her, a red dog that looked like an oversize hound took an attack position, growling low.

Yep. He'd forgotten how quick she was, and his recovery from a near panic attack had him at a disadvantage. He held his hands out to his sides, ribs aching. "It's me."

Eyes wide, she lowered her weapon, sliding it into her hip holster reflexively. "What's going on?" She reached toward him, hand hovering near his shoulder as though she wasn't sure he was real. "What's the danger?"

Ian took his first deep breath in what felt like days. "We need to get to shelter first. I've been hiding for an hour, and I'm not sure where they are." He dipped his chin toward the dog. "Can you call off the bodyguard?"

One hand motion reset the dog's demeanor. The animal sat, gaze on Meadow, waiting for the next command.

Ian watched as well. Meadow Ames was everything Ian had tried to forget. Her dark hair was up in a ponytail, which made her blue eyes even more haunting than his dreams remembered.

Ian shook away the thought. There was no time for a reunion, not with armed assailants stalking the woods. "Two shooters with pistols out here. Not sure where they went, but I know they're after me specifically." He could save the shocking revelation of who was stalking him for later. It was too much to get into when he wasn't sure how Silas and Des were alive. "How far away are you parked?"

The sky shook with thunder, and raindrops dotted the ground. Hopefully the noise would cover their escape.

Meadow turned, leading the way toward the creek. "I'm at the parking lot at the trailhead, so it's at least a half mile to—"

Up the hill to the left, the underbrush crashed. A cascade of rocks rolled down the slope and splashed into the creek.

Meadow whirled and ducked into the brush, dragging Ian down with one hand and the dog down with the other.

They crouched in the thicket, both listening. Even the dog's floppy ears were raised slightly. The animal lifted its nose and sniffed the air, still watching Meadow.

This was no ordinary dog. If he had to guess, he'd say Meadow had transferred to a K-9 unit, though her clothing and the dog's vest were nondescript, making it impossible to identify who she was affiliated with.

About a hundred yards away, something big moved through the brush, too close for comfort.

Meadow drew her sidearm.

Ian did the same.

The dog sat at attention.

"Hey, traitor!" The male voice rang through the trees, echoing off the mountain. It came from above and behind, not from where the initial rustlings were. "You can't stay out here all night. Might be better to take your chances with us than with whatever nature wants to throw at you."

It was clear neither Silas nor Des knew exactly where they were hiding, but the pair was closing in.

Ian and Meadow huddled deeper into the brush. At least it was summer and the foliage was thick. If it was winter, he'd already be dead.

Fat raindrops smashed cool against Ian's skin. The waning day and dark clouds left deep shadows. Still, if either of their assailants got too close, Ian and Meadow would be easy to spot.

To the left, the rustling drew nearer.

The dog growled low in her throat, a deep rumble that carried through the forest stillness.

The rustling stopped.

An explosion of sound flurried to the left and a woman— Des—yelled. "Bear! Get out!" Branches rattled and rocks rolled and bounced down the hill.

Overhead, thunder crashed and the sky opened up. A torrent of water seemed to fall all at once, the rain drowning out the sound of the fleeing assailants.

But not loudly enough to drown out a stream of expletives screamed from above. "We aren't leaving, Deputy! We know you're here!"

Despite the shouted threat, Des and Silas bolted, shadows in the rain, heading toward the logging road.

Meadow shoved her bangs out of her face. "What now? They aren't wrong about wild animals roaming around, and I also don't like the idea of trailing those two when we have no idea where they'll take cover."

Neither did he, and he had a better idea anyway. He'd been heading for shelter when Meadow had found him. "If you trust me, I know a place we can lie low until the storm passes and we can get some backup in here and get out. I'd say we're less than a mile from it."

"Sounds good to me. Lead the way."

The rain had already soaked them to the bone, and mud was rapidly making the ground more difficult to traverse. They made their way to the creek and crossed, hurrying along the thin open area at the bank as the rushing water greedily accepted the rain. At least the deluge would wipe away any trace of their path. Hopefully, it would keep up until they reached safety.

What felt like hours later, Ian gently slid vines and overgrowth to the side of a metal door built into the slope and flipped the dials on an all-weather padlock. He ushered Meadow into an old bunker then dragged the vegetation back over the opening and shut the door, shoving a huge bar into place to bolt it from the inside and hanging the padlock from a hook beside it.

The cavernous space was pitch-black and eerily silent after the roar of the rain. The air was stale and musty, but it was breathable. The ventilation fan had died long ago, but enough air leaked through the system to keep them alive.

A soft rustle, then a beam of light cut through the inky darkness as Meadow shone a flashlight. "Is this one of the old World War II bunkers?" She illuminated the ceiling, walls and floor of the space, which was about fifteen feet wide and thirty feet deep. Carved out of what was once a cave, the bunker had been built to provide shelter in case of attack during one of the most terrifying times in world history.

Ian reached for his cell phone, but it was no longer in his pocket. He turned a slow circle. Maybe he'd dropped it in—

Meadow held out her hand, his cell phone in her palm. "I found it in the brush. It's how Grace tracked you, but I'm pretty sure it's a brick now."

He inspected the device then tossed it onto a metal table.

How was he going to get in touch with his cousin if his phone was toast?

That was a worry for later. He'd have to survive if he wanted to find out what had frightened Brooke. "Shine your light to the back wall." Ian strode deeper into the space, following her illuminated path, and opened a metal cabinet anchored to the rear wall. He dug out a small oil hurricane lantern and waterproof matches, quickly lighting the lamp to dispel the darkness.

Meadow moved her thumbs over her phone's screen, then grimaced. "I've got zero signal in here."

"I normally get a bar or two, but the rain must be hindering the signal."

"Maybe." Meadow looked around the room. "How did you know this was here?"

Sliding the lantern to the center of the table, Ian glanced around the space he'd hoped to never see again. "Remember how, when I was undercover, I told you I had a place to go where no one could find me?" He held out his hands and turned slowly as if showing off a brand new vacation home. "Here we are. Chateau Carpenter, the envy of billionaires the world around."

Meadow sniffed what sounded like a short laugh, then let the dog off of the leash so she could explore the space. Sliding a backpack from her shoulders, she surveyed the room. "You stocked this place?"

"A few canned goods. A few sets of clothes. A go bag. Just enough to get by for a few days if I ever had to get out quick." He jerked a thumb toward a second metal door in the back wall. "There's a smaller room back there where I stashed my gear. You can go in there and change into something dry. The clothes will definitely be too big for you, but it's better than sitting around and freezing in wet jeans."

"I keep clothes in my backpack." She eyed him as though she was about to say something more...or as though she couldn't believe she was actually standing in his presence.

"Yes?" They'd always been honest with each other in the past. It had been a requirement if he wanted to survive his time undercover. He nearly hadn't, but that wasn't her fault. She'd done all she could to protect him. If she was thinking things now, he wanted to hear them.

"Just getting adjusted to seeing you."

Ian sucked in air through his teeth. As he had settled into his new life in Texas, carving out a space where he was comfortable and safe in more ways than one, his colleagues had been left in the dark. His disappearance into WITSEC and his decision not to return when the threat was over had likely gone unnoticed by his blood family, but Meadow...

She'd definitely noticed.

He'd considered reaching out, but it was better for both of them if he kept his distance. They'd parted as friends. She didn't need to know she'd haunted his dreams.

And he didn't need to entertain any illusions there could ever be something between them. Once she knew him well, she'd realize he wasn't worth the effort, and he couldn't handle that kind of heartbreak. There had been more than enough abandonment in his life.

Still, he owed her an apology.

Before he could speak, she called to the K-9, who trotted to her side. Meadow walked into the back room, shutting the door behind them.

The past hour had been a shock for both of them. Neither of them had awakened assuming the day would end with them together in an abandoned bunker after shots were fired.

Shots fired. At him. A nightmare he'd never wanted to

relive. Terror had paralyzed him flat to the ground in the brush, almost costing him his life.

It had taken long minutes for the panic attack to subside, long minutes in which Des or Silas could have found him and ended him.

Yet they hadn't.

Ian went to the exterior door and checked the bolt, his jaw tight. It was almost enough to make him believe God actually cared.

Almost. But not quite. People liked to talk about God being a Father, but fathers and mothers were unreliable and cruel. He wanted no more of that. God. The Creator was easy to believe in. Jesus and salvation? Sure. That was for the whole world. But a God who cared specifically and personally about him?

Nah. Nobody cared that much about him, no matter what the guys who'd led chapels on the rodeo circuit had said.

No matter that Meadow Ames had once made him imagine, for only a moment, that someone might.

Texting her was a mistake. He should have handled this himself.

He should have told her to bring reinforcements.

He should have done a lot of things.

But he hadn't, and now, not only was his life on the line, but he'd dragged Meadow right alongside him into danger.

The backup hiking pants and athletic shirt she kept in her day pack had saved her more than once. Ruefully, she inspected a few scratches on her arms before pulling her sleeves down over them. Given the terrain they'd crossed, she was grateful there were only a couple of small cuts.

Well, what was done was done. She hung her clothes on hooks along the wall. They wouldn't dry completely in this damp, enclosed space, but they might be less soaked by the time she crammed them into her pack again.

By the light of her flashlight, she surveyed the room. The space hollowed out of the mountain was an arch covered by corrugated aluminum and supported by thick metal poles. While the outer room held built-in shelves and a metal table and chairs, this one had metal bunks built into the wall. Ian had tossed a couple of blankets and some clothes in vacuum-sealed bags onto the bed frames. Otherwise, the room was empty.

She glanced at her phone. Still no signal. If she could reach Rocco for backup, she'd feel a whole lot better. There was no telling how long he'd wander around before he figured out she was "missing" and tracked her vehicle.

Until then, she and Ian were on their own.

With no way of knowing who was taking potshots at Ian or where they were, leaving this safe haven would be foolish.

She pulled the band from her ponytail, squeezed out the water and tied her hair back again.

Her hand stopped halfway through the motion.

The person in the woods had called Ian *traitor. Deputy.* Her eyebrows drew together. Either someone from his past had spotted him, or someone connected to the Thornton family knew he'd returned to the area.

But anyone from the op who'd want him dead was dead themselves.

And why was Ian in the area in the first place?

She shoved her phone into a pocket on her pants and headed to the outer room.

Ian had pulled the light jacket off and was inspecting his hands, which bore scratches of their own. He looked up when she came in. "Feel better?"

"I do." She was more concerned about him. Ian had nearly

been killed over a year and a half ago when Ronnie Thornton managed to pull some strings from prison. Being pursued by gun-toting assailants today had to have taken its toll. "Did they shoot at you?"

He studied his hands carefully in the thin light, his expression tense. "They shot at a rabbit I spooked out of the bushes." His voice was strained.

Meadow waited, but he offered nothing more. Plenty of people who'd suffered the kind of pain and recovery he'd endured had lingering PTSD. Had he frozen in the woods? Panicked?

He'd taken a bullet to the torso and lost his spleen shortly after their investigation concluded, courtesy of one of Ronnie's henchmen, prompting federal authorities to offer him protection until the trial and beyond. Sitting vigil in the waiting room of the hospital while Ian fought for his life wasn't a memory Meadow cherished.

It wasn't one she wanted to think about now either. "Something wrong with your hand?"

"Got a splinter in my palm. It'll work itself out."

"Let me see." She pulled a chair around and sat in front of him. "You have a first aid kit, I assume?"

He jerked his head toward the table, where a small plastic box rested.

Opening it up, Meadow donned gloves and retrieved tweezers and ointment. She took his hand. Even through the gloves, his skin was warm.

Focusing on the splinter instead of the man, she cleared her throat. "You pack a thorough first aid kit."

"I was a medic in the army before I was a deputy." He flinched as she dug the tweezers in.

Yet another little tidbit she hadn't known about the man she'd once cared about and maybe even…

No. That was the past. She'd never told him her feelings. He'd repeatedly spoken of his aversion to dating and marriage, of how he planned to live life as a bachelor. His family trauma ran deep, so Meadow had worked hard to guard her heart against any growing feelings. Obviously, his own heart had been as cold as he'd always said, or he'd have reached out to her after Ronnie died. As much as touching him sent a *zing* through her veins, she needed to focus on now. Developing or growing feelings for a man who would never return them would only lead to heartache.

Meadow worked quickly, removing the splinter and applying ointment. Pulling off the gloves inside out, she dropped them on the lid of the kit. "All done."

"Thanks." Stiffly, Ian stood and walked away, shutting the door to the rear room behind him. When he came back, he was dressed in a black hooded sweatshirt and sweatpants. He sat at the table and repacked the first aid kit. "You have questions." He glanced at her and almost smiled, the shadows of the lantern flickering across his face. "I can tell because your personality right now is…" He ran his hand palm-down through the air, as though she'd flatlined. "I know you. You're louder and more take-charge than this."

Meadow rested her hands on the cold metal table. "I don't even know where to start." The question burning her throat was the last one she'd ask. *With Ronnie dead, you were free to come out of hiding. Why didn't you reach out?*

The only conclusion was that he hadn't stayed away because of his safety, but because of her.

They'd been acquaintances before his undercover mission and had grown into friends during it. The least he could have done would have been to let her know he was safe and well when the threat went away.

Except, perhaps the threat hadn't died. "Who was stalk-

ing around in the woods? They called you *Deputy. Traitor.*
Somebody from your past? Before the Thornton op drove
you into hiding?"

"If only." Ian shook his head. "It was Silas and Des."

Meadow sat back hard against the chair. *Impossible.* "Silas
and Des are dead. There's DNA to prove it."

"We had teeth and a toe. Not hard to sacrifice those if
you're desperate to evade capture. It's possible the explosion that we thought killed them wasn't an accidental deto-
nation but was part of an escape plan Silas and Des had set
up from the start. After all, they led us to that warehouse.
They controlled the chase. Maybe we followed them where
they wanted, and we believed what they wanted us to believe.
Maybe they've been lying low, waiting for me to return."

If she didn't sound like herself, neither did he. Ian had
always had a swagger about him, a brash recklessness that
rode the edge of dangerous. It was one of the reasons she'd
suggested him for the undercover op.

Now he was subdued. Quiet.

For the first time, she took a good look at him. During the
op, he'd worn a beard and had kept his hair long. He must
have gone for the clean-shaven look in his new life. He currently sported a five-o'clock shadow, and his brown hair was
shorter, tousled on top where he'd hand-dried it after their
dash through the rain.

But his eyes… They were still a striking blue, although
stress had carved lines at the corners that weren't there before. The story of his difficulties undercover and his dance
with death were etched there.

She wanted to comfort the friend he'd been, but after
over a year and a half of zero communication, he was an
odd combination of confidant and stranger. She wasn't sure
what to do with that, so she sat with her hands clasped on

the cold metal, trying to digest what was happening. "Are you sure it was them?"

"I saw them both, plain as could be." He pushed away from the table and stood, pacing to the wall. Running his hand down the back of his hair, he stared at a shelf containing several large plastic boxes. "I should have been more careful."

"Careful of what? Who would have suspected that two dead people would come after you?" How had this happened? DNA from teeth and a toe had indicated Ronnie Thornton's son and second-in-command had died in that explosion along with his enforcer. So many questions. Either someone involved with the investigation was dirty or…

She shuddered to think much further, although Ian had hinted at it earlier. Silas had been identified by a toe recovered at the scene. Des by two teeth. The explosion had been so violent that very little else remained. It was possible they'd…

She shuddered at the idea someone would mutilate themselves in order to avoid arrest. But when it was life in prison versus life without a toe? She wouldn't put it past either of them. "So what really happened in that warehouse?"

Ian shrugged. "Who knows? Like I said, it could have been a fallback plan all along. They led us to that warehouse, so it could have been an elaborate setup."

"But how did they find you?"

"I have no idea. I thought it was safe to come back, at least for a few days."

Even though he'd stayed away initially. "Why come back now?" *Without telling me?*

"My cousin Brooke reached out. She thinks a friend is in trouble and asked me to poke around before she reaches out to the authorities in case she's wrong."

"Your cousin?" Meadow purposely infused her voice with confusion. In the hospital, while he was medicated and out of his head with pain, he'd told her awful stories about his family. But when he'd been fully awake, he'd shown no recollection of revealing his secrets. She'd pretended ignorance until the day he'd vanished. Out of respect for his privacy, she'd maintain the pretense now. "You always told me, told everyone, that you don't have any living relatives."

"Aside from my cousin, there are none who want to claim me and none I want to claim." He cleared his throat and resumed his seat. "I always kept in touch with one cousin. Brooke. She's twelve years younger than me, just turned nineteen. Always looked up to me for some reason." He stared at the table, tapping his finger on the corner of the first aid kit. "When I walked away and joined the army, she was the only one who wrote. The only one who cared. She was just a kid, but she made the effort and never stopped."

Meadow didn't know how to respond to his obvious pain.

Ian finally met her gaze, his expression almost tortured. "When Ronnie died, I reached out to her. Told her I was alive and was staying in Texas, where I was working with a vet to rehab horses for the rodeo circuit. I liked it there. I had friends. It was a new start, away from here and from the family who'd hurt me." His gaze flicked away from her and then back. "I should have told her to talk to the cops about her friend. I shouldn't have come back."

"You didn't know about Silas and—"

"Still. I should have been more careful. And now I've dragged you into it." His eyebrows drew together. "I never should have called you. It put you in the line of fire and—"

"Never apologize for asking for help." This time, she dared to touch him. Reaching across the table, she rested her hand on his. "I once promised to be by your side until the end, and it's not over yet, so here I—"

The door rattled and something crashed against it.

They both rose, and Grace leaped up, growling low at the door. Meadow hissed a command that caused her partner to sit, then reached for her pistol as a muffled voice drifted through the metal barrier.

"If you're in there, Deputy, you're not coming out alive."

THREE

Ian clamped down on angry words he never said anymore. He might not be sure God actually cared about him, but he did recognize his need to respect the Almighty's rules. He'd given up a lot of things the year before when he'd started going to chapel on the rodeo circuit, but his mouth had proven the toughest thing to tame, especially under stress.

Right now, *stress* was all he had.

Something pounded against the door. "You should know by now we won't give up."

Meadow and Ian whipped toward each other. They were at the disadvantage in this game. Des and Silas knew they were somewhere in the vicinity, though they might be guessing about their presence in the bunker. Meadow and Ian had no intel, no way of reaching the outside world. Ian had backed them into a corner.

Worse, he'd backed *Meadow* into a corner.

Given his background in law enforcement, getting them into this predicament was inexcusable.

She grabbed his wrist and whispered, "This is not your fault."

Ian tightened his grip on his pistol and balled his other fist, tugging from her grasp. That was debatable, but not at the moment.

Together, by some unspoken signal, they crept to the door. The voices outside were muffled but audible, discussing their strategy.

"You can't be sure he's in there." Des's voice was smooth as silk, a slight Creole Louisiana accent threading through the words.

"Where else would he be?" As much as Silas looked like he'd swaggered straight out of a *Sopranos* episode, his accent was all Lower Alabama. He cultivated a look and persona designed to make people underestimate him, but he was deviously intelligent. If he was ever seen bumbling around, it was to throw his prey off balance. "Know what? I'm not hanging around out here too long waiting on him to show himself. It's getting dark, and I don't have a rifle on me to handle bear. Or other big game."

There was no response. Likely, Des was close to the door, listening for movement. The dim lantern light didn't reach that far, but any noise above breathing would likely pass through the minuscule gaps around the metal door.

Never had Ian heard his own breaths so clearly. He tried to keep them shallow. A few feet away, Meadow did the same. She looked at him, gun low and at the ready. He'd trusted her with his life before, and here he was doing it again.

Only this time, hers was in his hands as well.

"We'll come back tomorrow," Des finally said. If they were leaving, that would give Meadow and him time to—

"But we're sealing off the door in case he's really in there."

Meadow met his eye and winced.

Des was crafty. Silas had always been the business-minded one while Des was the tactical one. Outside, metal screeched on metal. A former New Orleans cop, Des still carried handcuffs as her quick way of restraining anyone who got in her way. Likely, she'd threaded those cuffs through the holes for the padlock to lock the entrance.

Someone pounded on the door. Silas's voice followed. "See you in the morning, traitor."

The sounds of movement faded, and Ian's shoulders sagged.

With two fingers, Meadow motioned for him to follow. She walked through the bunker and into the back room, as far as they could get from the door. "Thoughts?"

"We're stuck in here until they come back."

"*If* they come back." She stared toward the main entry, her face a mask of determination. "They weren't certain we're here. Pretty sure all of the blustering was a test to see if we'd react." She checked her phone then shoved it into her pocket, clearly frustrated with the lack of signal. "Plan?"

"They can't get in here without some serious power tools. This place was designed to withstand a bomb blast. It might be old, but it's solid. I made sure when I first set it up as a refuge. We've got enough food and water for a week. We won't run out of oxygen because the air…"

Air.

Their ticket to an escape. "I know how to get out of here, but we'll have to wait until dark." Ian pointed to a wall-mounted fan near the top bunk, less than two feet square. "You aren't claustrophobic are you?"

"Nope." She followed the line of his finger. "Ventilation system?"

"It leads to the outside, and hopefully the opening hasn't been buried by a rock slide. The fact we're breathing says it's at least partially open." Hopefully it was also hidden enough to keep Silas and Des from finding it. If either of them thought long and hard, they'd realize the shaft existed. If they didn't already know, they'd definitely figure it out by morning.

Meadow was already climbing the bunk, her partner sitting patiently to the side. "Screwdriver?"

"Will a knife work?" He passed his pocketknife to her. She opened it and made quick work of removing the fan. "Kill the lantern. We don't need light leaking out."

Ian obeyed, then felt his way back in the pitch-dark that hung heavy in the bunker. Near Meadow, the inky blackness was softer, though he wouldn't call it light.

After a moment, Meadow's flashlight lit and she descended from the bunk. "It's open, though I can't see the end. There's light coming from somewhere. As soon as it's dark, I'll make my way out and pray they aren't standing there waiting."

"No doubt." It was their only shot, or he wouldn't send her through alone. Given the width of his shoulders, he'd never be able to make the crawl without getting wedged into place.

That and, though he'd never admit it, small spaces weren't his favorite.

Meadow brushed past him and went into the main room. The lantern lit shortly after. "Now, we wait."

When Ian followed, she had already retaken her seat at the table. "Should be full dark in a little less than an hour. I'll have to orient myself once I get through and pray I'm not coming out on the side of a sheer rock face."

True. He sat across from her. "Hungry? I could at least play host. There's some canned ravioli around here."

She smiled. "Childhood favorite?"

Definitely not. There were very few things he wanted to carry forward from his childhood, and he certainly didn't want to talk about his past. Instead, he jerked his chin toward the K-9 resting on a blanket in the corner. "What's up with your new partner?"

"Her name's Grace." Her voice stretched as she looked over her shoulder at the dog, who raised her head at the sound of her name. "After your op, I asked to become a K-9 handler again. That's what I did before I joined the task force that you were on. I was feeling a little…lost, so I reached out to one of my mentors from when I was first in, Sully Briggs. He reminded me how much I loved having a K-9 partner. I'm on the fugitive task force now, when I'm not working with the Mountain Country K-9 Unit to catch the Rocky Mountain Killer. Grace is a tracker, which is a good thing, or else I might not have found you." She turned to face him. "Tell me how you wound up in the woods today."

"Not much to tell." If anyone but Brooke had asked him to return, he'd have ignored the request. "My cousin works at one of the diners in Cattle Bend while she's going to community college. I'm supposed to meet with her in the morning, but I thought I'd cruise by and check on her before then. I'd just parked on the street in front of the diner when this Charger came up and basically aimed right at me. I didn't know who it was at first, just took off with them in pursuit. It wasn't until I was in the underbrush that I saw them and figured it out. How they knew I was coming into town, I have no idea. It could have been sheer coincidence they spotted me, but I don't know."

He'd thought it was safe to return. He'd been wrong.

"It's odd, for sure." Meadow twirled her phone on the table. She often fidgeted when she was thinking through a problem, a quirk he remembered from working with her. He'd always thought it was cute, though Meadow was too tough to be labeled *cute*. "With Ronnie dead, you're no longer considered a protected witness, but your identity and location remain classified as long as you wish. Maybe they lay low, gambling you'd come back home once you believed you were safe?"

"Maybe, but I don't consider this home."

"They don't know that." She looked up, seeming to try to make sense of his statement, but then her gaze shifted. "There's something else it could be." Meadow laid her palm on his busted phone. Her forehead creased. "I'm working on a serial-killer case out of Elk Valley, Wyoming, but one of the murders happened in Glacierville. We were at the PD going over files, and I heard some of the officers talking about how several young people have gone missing over the past four months in the surrounding counties. All late teens or early twenties. Beyond being concerned for their safety, I didn't give it much tactical thought, but—"

"But that's the age group the Thorntons targeted when they were operational as human traffickers." Ian planted his elbow on the table and rubbed the bridge of his nose. "Silas and Des must be starting the operation again. We're close enough to Missoula that they may have assets here that weren't seized in the initial investigation." He felt sick to his stomach, and it had nothing to do with hunger. "They're rebuilding their 'inventory.'" How many young men and women would fall prey to people who treated them as merchandise to be auctioned off to the highest bidder?

This shouldn't be happening. "We shut them down." The words ground out through clinched teeth. He'd been undercover for months and had nearly died bringing the Thornton syndicate to justice. The idea they were back, preying on the vulnerable…

He shoved away from the table and paced the room, feeling caged. "We have to get out of here. We've got to alert local law enforcement and our old task force—"

"Right now we have to be patient." Meadow's demeanor was calm, but her eyes were determined.

He knew that look, and he hated it. She was prepared for patient waiting.

Ian wanted to take action. To charge out and apprehend Silas and Des before they could continue an operation that would leave behind a horrifying path of physical and emotional destruction.

Meadow crouched on the top bunk, the metal cold against her knee, and shoved her head into the pitch-black darkness of the airshaft. She didn't dare use her flashlight. If Silas and Des were skulking nearby, light would draw them like moths, and they'd be waiting with guns drawn when she emerged.

She closed her eyes and breathed deeply. There were more immediate concerns, however.

Spiders. Snakes. Creepy-crawly critters.

Literally anything could be lurking in the metal tube that offered their only route to escape, and she'd be crawling along the unfamiliar passage blind. Small spaces didn't bother her, but unseen spiders?

She swallowed against her gag reflex. *Lord, help me.*

Flight instinct made every muscle in her body rebel against the darkness. She didn't look back at Ian, who was keeping Grace occupied. If she did, she'd morph into a full-blown, feather-covered chicken. One step back would mean zero steps forward.

And she had to move forward.

It had been a long wait for full darkness, plenty of time for her mind to weave monster spider webs. The sooner she plunged in to face whatever dwelled in the dark, the sooner she'd be out in open air.

With one more prayer that definitely wouldn't be her last, she hefted herself into the narrow space and stretched out on her belly. A barely there breeze brushed her skin, raising the hair on her arms. She reached out her hands, exploring the damp, cold metal ahead of her.

A bulbous *something* scraped beneath her fingertips.

Meadow gasped, whacking her head against the metal roof. *Ew. Ew. Ew.*

I don't want to do this. The refrain looped through her thoughts. A shaky breath and a prayer forced a reset on the mantra. *I* can *do this.*

If she didn't, they were dead. Silas and Des could return with dozens of thugs. Their best chance at survival was flight.

But...spiders...

Terror squeezed her lungs. She slid her fingers over the bump and found a series of them. Rounded metal rivets ran across the floor where the metal had been pieced together. Okay, so she knew what those were.

Somehow, the evidence that the bumps were all man-made loosened the vise around her lungs.

"You okay?" Ian's whisper wafted to her.

"Good." She kept her answer short, not certain how far the metal tube would carry sound. On grit and prayer, she inched forward, farther from the light and deeper into the unknown.

Meadow closed her eyes, seeking a sense of control. She had no way to judge how far she'd traveled or how far she had to go. Without gravity holding her to the floor, she wouldn't have been sure which way was up or forward. Her mind swirled, disoriented.

The barely moving air tickled her arms, mimicking a thousand spiders' feet.

Meadow gagged on fear.

Her jaw convulsed, knocking her teeth together. She wanted to dig her fingernails into her arms and scratch until the sensation went away.

Only the small tactical part of her mind kept her moving forward, and it was shrinking rapidly.

A damp puff of air carried the scent of rain.

Had she reached the end?

Her eyes popped open, but there was only darkness.

Focus on the fresh air.

She set her face into the increasing breeze, fighting for inches. Maybe—

Something brushed her face.

Meadow squeaked a swallowed scream and dug her teeth into her lower lip. Staccato breaths burned her nose. She actually whimpered.

Whimpered.

Gulping air, she swiped at her face. A sticky cobweb clung to her fingers.

Oh, let it be an old cobweb and not an active web.

A thousand minuscule spider legs skittered across her skin. Real? Or imagined?

She shuddered. Her breaths came faster. *There's no way there are thousands of spiders in here.*

Or is there?

Meadow puffed air through pursed lips, trying to focus on anything else. Blue skies. Warm blankets. Training with Grace.

If only she knew where the end of this narrow shaft was.

The urge to stop and bury her face in her arms was real, but if she did, she'd never move again.

Sweeping her hands in front of her, Meadow pulled forward.

The cobwebs became more prevalent. Her heart rate picked up with each wispy, sticky contact.

Nausea built in her body with every move. She'd never had a panic attack before, but there was always a first time.

The air shifted, cooled. The breeze stiffened. The scent of rain grew stronger.

Meadow opened her eyes. The darkness seemed different

somehow. Softer? She still couldn't see her hand in front of her face.

Except…

Meadow waved her hand and a slight shadow moved.

Relief weakened her muscles until they shook. The end had to be near. There was no other way she was getting out without losing her mind.

A square of lighter darkness appeared.

The grate. Meadow pulled like she never had before, heedless of what might lie between her and freedom. She no longer cared. She just wanted out.

Her fingertips scraped metal grate, and she laced her fingers through it to move herself closer with a final burst of strength, holding her face inches from the opening, terrified to press her cheek against it for fear of a rogue spider's retaliation.

Freedom was eight metal screws away. *Lord, don't let this thing be rusted shut.*

She was not going backward down that metal tube of terror.

As her eyes adjusted to the dim light, she listened. Rain still fell, though it was a gentle shower now. The wind tousled the trees.

Only the sounds of nature reached her ears.

That didn't mean Silas and Des weren't lurking nearby.

As much as she'd hated the ventilation shaft, she'd reached the most dangerous part of her journey.

Every inch of her wanted to bash her way out, but removing the screws would take calm and steady hands. Ian had sent her forward with his pocketknife, so she felt for the screws and prayed the small screwdriver tool would hold up to the strain.

Swiping sweat from her palms onto her sleeve, Meadow took a deep breath and went to work. It felt like hours, but a few minutes later, she eased the last screw from its place and jerked the metal grate away from the opening. It scraped with a sound that had to be heard for miles.

Gently, she eased it against the wall beside her and slipped forward, sweeping vines away from the opening as she scanned the area. The light seemed so bright outside, though the moon and stars were obscured by clouds. The shaft's opening was in the side of a steep hill, about three feet up from the level ground below. High enough to avoid flooding, low enough for her to exit headfirst without hurting herself.

Meadow wanted to launch herself from her prison, but she waited, listening for movement that might indicate either Silas or Des had found the grate and were lying in wait.

There was no evidence of another human, though they could be hiding. If only she had Grace, who was a rock star at alerting to the presence of others.

Wriggling out of the shaft, Meadow extended her hands and caught herself on the ground, where she rolled onto her back and lay still, staring up at the clouds, which glowed dimly in the lights from nearby towns. Rain dotted her face, and she reveled in fresh air and freedom. She breathed mountain air for long moments before she finally felt strength in her bones...along with a sheepish blush over her spider scare.

She'd never confess that to anyone.

Carefully, using the soft glow from the clouds to guide her, she felt her way down the hill toward the bunker's door, wishing for her flashlight but wary of giving away her position if someone was tracking her. Neither Des nor Silas were the outdoorsy type, so she was hopeful the rain and the threat of wild forest animals had kept them away.

At the bottom of the hill, she crouched, listening. Other than the rainfall, the breeze in the trees and a few small rustles of night creatures in motion, no sound came to her.

Wary that a bullet could slam into her back at any moment,

she pulled her handcuff keys from the pocket she'd stashed them in, crept to the entrance and used the universal key to unlock Des's cuffs. She knocked three times lightly, paused, then knocked twice, Ian's signal to open the door.

The bolt slid back with a screech before the door eased open and Ian peeked out.

Meadow ducked through, and Grace was at her side immediately, licking her hand in greeting as she waited for a command. Meadow gave her a quick ear scratch, but her focus was on Ian. They couldn't waste time talking. "I think it's clear, but we should get moving. I don't trust them not to come back now that the storm has passed. Silas was never a patient one. If he suspects you're in here, he won't wait until morning to be sure."

Ian turned toward the table then stopped to study her in the lamplight. "You okay?"

"Just ready to move." She walked past him to gather her pack and Grace's things.

He swiped at her shoulder as she walked by.

Meadow froze. "Why?" She had suspicions, but boy, they'd better be wrong.

"No reason. We should get moving."

Ignoring the fear that powered through her, Meadow kept walking. The spider he'd swiped from her shoulder was the least of her worries.

Outside that door, the enemy could be waiting, and she needed to focus less on skittering critters and more on flying bullets.

FOUR

After extinguishing the lantern, Ian grabbed his things and followed Meadow.

At the door, she stopped and held a hand out to keep Ian from proceeding.

The last thing he wanted to do was wait. All he wanted was safety and security for her and her partner…and for himself. Those long minutes alone had brought too many opportunities for past pain and fear to play games with his head.

He never wanted a bullet to pierce his flesh again, yet here he was, tensed against that very thing.

Still, he knew better than to rush forward. "Did you hear something?"

"No." Meadow clipped a leash to her K-9's harness. "But Grace is trained to track, and she'll alert if she catches anyone's scent. There's a pretty stiff breeze, so they'd have to be upwind of us, but it's something. At least the wind is blowing from the direction of the parking lot where my SUV is and the logging road where your truck is."

"They're almost definitely watching my truck."

"Which is why we're heading for my vehicle first." She eased the door open and exited with Grace. "Hopefully, they haven't realized you're not alone."

At a soft command from Meadow, Grace lifted her head

and sniffed the air, seeming to scan in all directions before she returned her attention to Meadow to watch for her next command.

Even Ian knew that was good news.

Meadow exhaled slowly. "We're clear, at least in the direction we want to go. I can't promise they aren't somewhere downwind, but we'll take it slow. No flashlights. Keep quiet in case those two are roaming around looking for an opportunity."

The scar in his abdomen ached, though the sensation was all in his head. He'd spent a year and a half with his muscles tight, waiting for the slam of another bullet. None of that tension compared to the adrenaline-fueled pain of walking in almost total darkness through the woods with assailants on the hunt. He kept one eye on Grace, who constantly sniffed the air and the ground, and the other on where his next footfall would land.

He tried to keep his steps light as they crept along the creek bank, where it was easier to walk but they were slightly more exposed. All around, the woods and the creek talked, obscuring the sounds of anyone who might be sneaking up on them.

Every muscle in his body ached, reminders of a day that had nearly destroyed him.

Two days after Ronnie Thornton was led out of the courtroom where Ian's testimony had sealed his fate, the criminal had dished out his revenge. When Ian opened the door to his SUV at the sheriff's department to go on his first regular patrol after being undercover, a man had stepped from a vehicle on the street and opened fire.

Most of the bullets thwacked into Ian's SUV. One grazed his hip. The other scorched into his abdomen, slicing through his spleen before exiting out his back.

The pain hadn't hit instantly. Sheer adrenaline and training had driven Ian to return fire along with several other deputies in the lot at the time. But the world had suddenly dimmed and spun, and the last memory he had was dropping to his knees and looking down to see nothing but red. So much red...

Ian shook his shoulders to throw off the memory that still made his side ache and his head spin. Instead, he focused on keeping pace with Meadow, on the scent of rain-washed forest and the sounds of the night. All the things he'd missed in his new life in West Texas, where the air was dry and the land was parched.

Yes, he'd missed Meadow Ames. He'd denied it to himself for all of the months he'd been out of pocket, convincing himself he was happy working with the horses from the rodeo circuit and getting back in touch with the veterinarian dreams he'd had as a child.

But at night, when he laid his head down, no amount of sleep could make him forget her. It was unbelievably unprofessional to fall for your handler, and yet...he almost had.

That was the main reason he'd kept his distance after word came that Ronnie had been murdered, the victim of a homemade knife to the abdomen after he crossed the wrong man in prison. At the time, it had appeared the major players in the Thornton organization were dead, the minions in jail or scattered, and the threat to Ian's life was over.

He'd opted to remain in Texas with the new name of Zeke Donner and the new life he'd settled into, even if it fit like a shirt that was a size too small. It was safer for both himself and Meadow if he stayed in place and left her to live her life as she pleased.

Eventually, he'd move on, too.

Then the call had come from Brooke. His cousin was the

one person in his family who'd ever shown him affection or had cared whether he came or went. Sure, she was the youngest, but she was also the one who'd reached out when everything went wrong. She'd never blamed him for the accident that took her brother's life. Even though she was a child at the time, she'd been aware of Dean's addictions and failures. It was the rest of the family who'd vilified Ian and shoved him out…first for not making sure Dean didn't have keys the night he died and, second, for going into law enforcement, the profession that threatened their livelihood the most. They'd shut him out completely.

Not that life had ever been easy. The addictions and dysfunctions that led his mother and her sister to make money by any means necessary meant he'd never known what love and safety looked like. In fact, he'd met the wrong end of his mother's fists on more than one occasion, always refusing to fight back.

There was no way he would ever saddle a woman with the kind of baggage he carried or the deficiencies in his emotions. He was cold inside. That trait had made him a methodical law enforcement officer and perfect for the undercover job that had almost ended his life. It did not make him a good candidate for building a future or a family.

Though with Meadow… In the same way her name brought the image of grassy fields dotted with spring flowers, she'd once brought warmth to his heart.

The unfamiliar feeling had scorched his soul and left him in exquisite pain. Leaving her behind had been the right thing to do. If he'd had any other option today, he wouldn't have called her, but his life had depended on her once again.

And she'd thrown caution to the wind to protect him… once again.

"You still good back there?" Meadow's soft whisper

slammed the door on his thoughts. She glanced over her shoulder, the movement more visible now that his eyes had adjusted to the night.

He swallowed words that didn't need to be spoken. "Good."

They trudged up a slope now, having passed under the footbridge without him even noticing, and were headed toward the parking lot. Hopefully, no one was watching her vehicle. Ian was cold and still damp, even though he'd changed clothes. He was starving for more than a can of cold ravioli. And he desperately needed to find a place where Meadow Ames wasn't, before she fanned the embers in his heart to flame.

As they neared the parking area, Meadow slowed.

Ian fought the urge to move between her and whatever danger might lie ahead.

That would earn him a swift reprimand, he was certain. While he was a competent, highly trained law enforcement officer, Meadow's training and expertise with the US Marshals far exceeded his. She could run circles around him, but that didn't stop him from wanting to protect her.

Clearly, his heart was already in the danger zone.

The idea of what she might do if he suggested she couldn't take care of herself almost made him smile. It was the very reason he'd bitten his tongue in the bunker when she'd hefted herself into the ventilation shaft. She was afraid of spiders and all things creepy-crawly, but her bravery knew no bounds. It was one of the many things he admired about her.

They huddled in the underbrush at the edge of the gravel parking area with Grace between them. The dog sat, nose in the air, sniffing the breeze.

Meadow gave the K-9 a whispered command that Ian couldn't quite make out, and Grace instantly lay down, her paws straight out and her nose pointed ahead, ears perked.

Meadow looked over her partner's head and directly at Ian, her expression grim.

He didn't need to be trained with K-9s to understand what he was seeing. Grace was alerting.

Someone was nearby.

They waited silently in the bushes for what felt like hours.

Ian scanned the sky. A break in the clouds could spell disaster if the half-moon shone through. While it would allow them to see anyone searching for them, it would make them sitting ducks for sure.

The darkness at the wood line on the other side of the parking lot lit up, and it took all Ian had not to duck.

A face illuminated in the glow of a cell phone. As dim as she had her phone, Des still couldn't avoid being lit by the screen as she likely texted Silas, who was probably guarding Ian's truck.

They truly were trapped.

Meadow tapped his arm and pointed down the hill toward the creek.

Smart thinking. If they moved while she was staring at the screen or before her eyes adjusted to the darkness again, then they could avoid being seen. They trekked to the creek, crossed at the narrow spot where he'd hidden before and traversed about half a mile up the other side of the hill before they stopped behind a large boulder.

Meadow crouched behind the rock, shielding her phone with her hands. "I've finally got a signal, and I'm alerting backup. Otherwise, we're never getting out." Her fingers moved swiftly across the screen as she sent a text, then opened a map.

"You know, we could circle back and take Des into custody." It should have occurred to him sooner.

"These guys are out for blood. Des isn't the type to let

herself be spotted by accident. It could have been a trap. I don't like going in without intel when they could have their own backup waiting in the wings. Even if members of my team showed up, I'd be leery of attempting a takedown in the dark without knowing who else is out there."

True. But boy, did his feet itch to head back and put an end to this assault sooner rather than later. As long as Silas and Des were prowling around, he was in danger, and so was everyone he cared about.

Ian studied Meadow's phone screen upside down, then pointed to something in the corner. "There. There's another logging road."

"It's two miles away in the dark."

"We've got no other choice." Behind them lay a known route with an almost certain firefight at the end. Before them lay the unknown.

Either way, they were walking into danger.

It felt like they'd been walking for hours.

A thousand imaginary spiders still tiptoed across her skin. No matter how much she rubbed her arms, Meadow couldn't shake the sensation. Until she got into a well-lit place, had a shower, and changed into clothes not coated in cobwebs and dirt, there was no way she'd feel free of that ventilation shaft.

The mountain air was chilled and damp from the earlier rainfall. If they dared to stop, she'd pull her thin rain jacket on for the insulation, but with death prowling around searching for them, a pause could spell disaster.

They'd made their way up the hill, away from the creek, following a narrow trail while stepping carefully to avoid injuries. According to the map, the trail should lead to the logging road, or at least in its general direction. Meadow kept one eye on the ground vaguely illuminated by the half-moon that played peekaboo between the clouds, and one eye on Grace to see if her partner alerted to any odd scents.

So far, the K-9 seemed more interested in sniffing the ground than the air, so they were likely safe. She glanced at the phone screen only on rare occasions in an attempt to maintain cover and night vision. The alerts were shut off to prevent even the buzz of a silent alert from giving away their location. They were headed in the right direction, but discerning how much ground they'd covered was difficult given the uneven terrain and their irregular pace.

From a few steps behind, tension radiated off of Ian. He'd been silent since they set out. There was no doubt he was constantly scanning the area. He hadn't relaxed since they left the bunker.

His stress fed hers, and she needed to do something before the imaginary spiders and Ian's tension crawled through her skin.

When the trail widened, Meadow commanded Grace to heel, then slowed to allow Ian to step beside her. "We must be getting close. There's been more foot traffic through here. It's made a clearer trail."

"Yep."

Ian tended to be a take-charge guy. They'd butted heads a few times on his op, when she'd given direction and he'd wanted to do things his way. While he'd ultimately followed orders, sometimes it had been a pain to get him there. For him to be silently following along now meant he was lost in his head. "What's going on with you?"

He didn't slow his pace but kept moving along with her, looking right and left, up and down. His surveillance never stopped. "Ready to get out of here."

"And?"

"And what?"

The sounds of night creatures filtered between them. In the distance, two owls called to each other, the almost human cry sending a shudder through her bones.

Ian flinched, but his steps didn't stutter.

It wasn't like him to be skittish. He'd been a solid rock on his undercover op, never shying away from danger. Nothing scared him. Even the day he'd been shot, he'd taken down the man who—

The day he'd been shot.

That had to be the problem. The bullet that had torn through Ian's abdomen had come perilously close to ending his life. Having another gunshot in his vicinity today had definitely played on old fears. "You can still feel it hitting you, can't you?"

For the first time, Ian missed a step. He stumbled sideways, bumping her shoulder before he regained his footing. They walked in silence for so long, she was certain he was going to ignore the question.

They split around a tree in the center of the trail. When they rejoined one another, Ian finally spoke. "I didn't feel it hit." He sniffed and sped up slightly, as though he could outrun the past. "How did you know?"

"I'm an investigator. I made a deduction based on what I know about your personality and about your demeanor tonight."

She was several feet in front of him before she realized he'd stopped walking. When she turned, she was slightly higher up the trail, putting them eye to eye. In the thin, milky moonlight, his face was a blue shadow, but that didn't keep her from seeing he was looking right at her, studying her as though he was trying to solve a puzzle.

Even two years later, the pull toward him was real. The one she'd managed to shove aside and forget existed.

Until today.

His eyes narrowed as though he couldn't quite make out the words on a book's page. "You always did seem to know what I was thinking." The words were so quiet, he likely hadn't meant to say them out loud.

"Your expressions were always an open book. Anybody could read you." When he'd first gone undercover, she'd worried the Thorntons would see right through him, but he'd managed to convince them he was willing and able to be on their payroll.

He chuckled and almost smiled, then stepped around her and started to walk again. "No. Just you."

Was that true? Did she really know him better than anyone else?

Meadow remained behind Ian, letting him take point. He seemed to relax with her watching the rear.

He still trusted her to protect his blind spots.

So why hadn't he trusted her enough to reach out when Ronnie Thornton died?

She started to ask, then shoved the question aside. Trudging through the forest in the dark on a blind run for their lives wasn't the time to rehash the past or to air her emotional grievances.

They walked for what could have been ten minutes or an hour before Ian stopped and crouched on the trail, leaving room for her to join him. "Look."

She took a knee, and Grace obediently sat at her hip.

About ten yards up the trail, the light was different, as though the sky above opened up and allowed the moon full access.

It had to be the logging road. They'd hit straight on the clearing where she'd told Rocco to meet them.

The forest around them was completely silent. The night creatures had stilled.

Someone was nearby.

Lord, let it be Rocco.

Des and Silas were smart. They could read a map as well as she could. It was possible they'd called in backup to cover all potential escape routes.

"Think we've got bad company?" Ian's whisper sounded like a shout in the stillness.

She considered all of the scenarios. "Possibly, but I doubt it. If they had more manpower, they'd have had someone sitting on the bunker's entrance. There are a lot of logging and forestry service roads out here. There's no way they have enough people to cover them all." *Hopefully.* "Shield me while I see if Rocco has texted."

Meadow bent low to the ground beside Grace, letting the dog's body block the light.

Ian hunched protectively over her, completing a triangle that would hopefully shield the dim light of her phone from potential prying eyes. She gripped the device, focusing on the task at hand and trying to ignore how close Ian was. Closer than he'd ever been, she was sure.

What in the world was wrong with her? They were in danger. She certainly shouldn't be noticing how Ian's breath was warm on her cheek or that he somehow still smelled like soap and leather, even after the day he'd had.

She flicked the screen and a notification appeared.

Rocco. Nine minutes earlier.

Just arrived. All clear.

Meadow wanted to sink to the ground in relief. "He's here."

Ian's exhale swept across the base of her ponytail, flickering tendrils across her neck. "What are we waiting for?"

Meadow shook off the sensation of his presence. "Nothing." She let him move first because if she lifted her head, they'd be face-to-face. Frankly, in her relief, she might do something incredibly foolish.

She needed sleep. Lots of sleep, because her tactical brain was rapidly checking out in favor of her hidden guilty-pleasure heart that liked rom-coms and sappy romance novels.

She ought to read more spy stories, clearly.

It took a moment for Ian to move, but he stood slowly, turning toward the trail.

He knew better than to offer her a hand up. She'd broken him of that habit early on. She was capable of taking care of herself.

Though she knew Rocco was near, she eased around Ian and drew her sidearm, making a clicking sound against her teeth to draw Grace to her side.

With her partner at heel, she crept forward, scanning the trees and the pine-needle-covered road as they approached.

At the edge of the clearing, the hulk of an SUV silently waited.

Rocco.

They were out of the woods…

But the threat to Ian's life had just begun.

FIVE

"Welcome to Casa de Ames." Meadow opened the door to the small home about half an hour outside of Glacierville and ushered Grace inside, mimicking Ian's earlier grandiose pronouncement.

The K-9 bolted through the living area and straight for the open kitchen at the back of the house, diving headfirst into a massive water bowl.

Rocco's K-9, a chocolate Lab named Cocoa, scrambled across the hardwood toward Grace as soon as Rocco released her.

Ian chuckled. He'd seen horses behave similarly after long rehab sessions. Only hydration and home mattered.

Meadow dropped her gear onto a bench by the door, and Rocco did the same before he headed for the fridge. He tossed a bottle of water to Meadow then turned to Ian. "Want something?"

Ian nodded and caught the bottle Rocco threw to him, but something ugly crawled through his stomach. Officer Rocco Manelli was awfully comfortable in Meadow's home. So was his K-9 partner.

Draining her water bottle as she walked, Meadow crossed the living room, headed for a hallway on the opposite side of the house. "I'm going to clean up. You guys are on your own." She disappeared, and seconds later, a door shut.

"What was that about?" Rocco pulled two dog bowls from the pantry and fed the K-9s.

Yeah, he was definitely too comfortable. "What was what about?"

"Meadow running off before she even looks after Grace? It's not like her."

So, Ian knew something about Meadow that Rocco didn't. *Interesting.* "She's deathly afraid of spiders, but she doesn't think I know. I flicked one off of her shoulder after she came out of the ventilation shaft. I'm guessing she's been feeling them all over her since she made her way out."

"Spiders, huh? She's been hiding that little phobia from all of us." Rocco finished feeding the animals and refilled their water bowls. He poured a glass of juice, then poked around in the fridge. The man was constant motion. "You hungry?"

Ian didn't feel this at ease in his own apartment, let alone in someone else's home. It was clear Rocco was familiar with the place and comfortable taking whatever he needed. Was he here often? Were he and Meadow…a couple?

The thought curled his lip, slithering a thread of dislike for Rocco through him.

But Ian had no claim on Meadow, and this man had saved their lives. Whatever he was feeling had to be exhaustion or an adrenaline crash. Nothing more. He needed a redirect and fast.

Food should do the trick. "I could eat." Ian walked to the island that separated the living room from the kitchen. "Thanks for putting yourself in harm's way to get us out of there."

"It's what we do." Rocco shrugged and slammed the fridge door, then opened the freezer. "Meadow is the worst grocery shopper in the world. The only thing she has is frozen food. Pizza good?"

Actually, frozen pizza sounded like a gourmet meal. "At this point, I'll eat whatever you find. Canned ravioli didn't hold me."

"Been there, done that." Rocco tossed three frozen pizzas onto the counter and started the oven, then pulled plates from the pantry. "Near-death experiences tend to amp up the appetite."

Nodding slowly, Ian surveyed the room, trying not to think about Meadow cuddling on the couch with or, worse, kissing Rocco. So what if they were dating? Good for both of them if they were. Rocco seemed like a good guy, and Ian wasn't the man Meadow needed.

Though it hadn't stopped him in the past from wishing he could be. And it didn't stop green sludge from running through his veins now.

Seeking distraction, he scanned Meadow's home. The hardwood floors were dark, and scattered colorful rugs broke up the space. There was no dining room table, just the huge island with comfy stools where he currently sat. The walls were a soft gray, making the space feel cool and comfortable. The living area held a brick fireplace painted white and a nap-worthy blue couch with a matching love seat and side chairs. It was immaculate, the result of a trait he'd come to recognize in Meadow.

"Meadow's got a guest room, and she's also got a twin bed in her office. We'll crash here tonight and make a game plan in the morning." Rocco leaned against the counter by the stove and crossed his arms over his chest. "Any idea how these two seemed to come back from the dead to target you?"

"I'm sorry." Rocco knew way too much about Meadow's home life, and Ian couldn't focus on anything else. Either exhaustion or shock had worn away his filter. "Are you and Meadow dating?"

Rocco's arms fell to his sides, and he almost sputtered like an old Saturday-morning cartoon character.

Meadow's laugh sounded from behind Ian. "You're kidding, right? Me and Rocco?"

Ian didn't dare turn toward her. He could feel the back of his neck flaming. The red was probably spreading to his face, too. He should have kept his mouth shut.

"Hang on, hang on." Rocco walked to the island and leaned forward to watch Meadow as she walked into the kitchen. "You scoff like I'm not a serious catch." He held out his hands and turned a slow circle. "I've got it all. Brains, beauty—"

"An ego the size of the state of Wyoming." The sarcasm dripped from Meadow's words. She shoved Rocco aside and walked into the kitchen, then poured a glass of juice. She'd changed into leggings and an oversize black sweatshirt that said Yes, I'm Cold. Her damp hair hung to her shoulders, and her cheeks were slightly red from either the heat of the shower or the scrubbing she'd given them.

Time to change the subject. "Did you rinse all of the spiders off?"

She pointed a finger at Ian. "Shut your sound, pal. I'd rather forget that trek through Arachnophobia Land ever happened. It was all sunshine and rainbows as far as my memory is concerned." She pulled out the stool at the end of the counter and arched an eyebrow at him. "And *why* would you think I was dating *Rocco*?"

"You say my name like it's an ugly word." Rocco looked up from shoving pizza in the oven. "Once again, I have to ask why the idea is so repulsive."

"Dude, we'd be *Rocco* and *Meadow*. That's way too much greeting-card rhyme for me." With a heavy sigh, Meadow rolled her eyes and pivoted to face Ian. "So…why?"

He knew he looked like a deer caught in the headlights. He could feel his eyes widen. He was too tired and drained to come up with a quip. "I guess..." He guzzled his water and set the bottle on the counter. "It seems like he spends a lot of time here, so I assumed..." That sounded so juvenile. Totally like a middle-school boy. They were both going to crack up laughing at his expense.

Instead, Meadow nodded, her face growing serious. "That's because he *is* here a lot."

"In a professional capacity." Rocco threw a stack of napkins onto the island between Meadow and Ian. "Most of the team is. We're investigating a multistate serial-killer case, and one of our crime scenes is in Glacierville."

"The team bunks here if they need an overnight. It's more comfortable than a hotel, I hope." Meadow grinned. "But it probably does look weird to an *outsider*." She smirked.

Outsider. He'd used the code name in his text to her earlier, and she was letting him know she remembered.

"I heard that tone. Outsider?" Rocco rested his elbows on the island and leaned toward them, his dark eyes sparking with mischief. "What's that about?"

Meadow chuckled. "Your story, Carpenter."

It was. And it was better than talking about how he'd believed Rocco was comfortable at Meadow's house for all the wrong reasons. "It was the code name for the operation I was undercover on, the one that got me into this mess today." They needed to discuss what had happened, but Rocco had been right earlier. Food and rest came first so they could attack the situation later with clear heads. "That's it."

"That's so not *it*." Now that she was definitely spider-free, Meadow's true personality was shining through. The touch of mischief that often sparked when she was tired and her guard was down had flared to life.

"We don't have to tell this part." Because, yeah, he needed more embarrassment.

Rocco's eyebrow arched, and he leaned even closer, as though he had a secret to share. "I feel like we do."

"Oh, we do." Meadow sipped her juice. "The joint task force wanted someone to go under with the Thorntons in Missoula, and we tapped Ian, who was a deputy sheriff for Peak County but unlikely to be recognized in Missoula. His first meeting with our team was a working lunch at my office, and he—"

"And I managed to hit the table and knock over four of the six drinks sitting there. Meadow's fell right into her lap." He was taking charge of this story before she could embellish it. "For some reason, she thought it was cute to call me *Soda* after that."

Rocco's brows knit together. "And *Soda* led to *Outsider* because... Oh." He nodded and backed away from the counter, standing tall. "The book we all had to read in school. *The Outsiders.* One of the brothers is named—"

"Soda." Meadow laughed. "As a code name for an op, *Outsider* sounded a lot better than *Soda.*"

Lacing his fingers behind his head, Ian leaned back in his chair. "And a legend was born."

"In your own mind." Meadow popped him in the ribs and stood. "So anyway, that's how Ian got his code name, and that's why Rocco knows my house so well. Any more questions?"

Yeah, he had more, especially if talking would distract him from the way he shivered when she touched him. "If Rocco is a cop from Elk Valley—" a fact he'd dropped on the ride to Meadow's house "—and you're still with the Marshals out of Missoula, this unit you're in must be interesting. Can you talk about it?"

Meadow looked at Rocco, and they seemed to have a silent conversation before coming to a decision as the oven timer went off. She waited for the beeps to stop. "We can tell you a big chunk about it, but strap in… It's a wild one."

Meadow watched while Rocco sliced the square pizzas into quarters. It was no surprise Ian had wondered about a relationship between them. Most of the team ran around her house like they owned the place since they spent so much time investigating in Glacierville.

She didn't want to think about the way Ian had asked the question, as though he had a vested interest in the answer. He'd almost seemed…jealous? Not in a creeptastic way, but in a way that warmed her heart.

Ian had always been attractive, with his carefully tousled light-brown hair and blue eyes that saw straight into her thoughts. They'd connected when they'd worked together and had built a friendship. Outside of the op, what would a relationship have looked like? If they'd met at the grocery store, would the same *click* have happened?

Things had certainly *clicked* for her. At some point in their off-the-grid meetings and in the aftermath of his near-death experience, she'd fallen hard for him.

Because of past family issues, it was a feeling he would never reciprocate, so she'd buried the emotion, layering on dirt after he vanished into WITSEC.

Clearly, she hadn't buried it deep enough. Even though he'd shut all doors on any sort of romantic future together, his failure to reach out after Ronnie died cut.

His reappearance today created a storm in her head and her heart.

Having him in her home made her wonder how it would

have been simply to have dinner together. Watch TV together. Be normal people who had a chance at—

"You know I hate this." Rocco slid a plate onto the bar in front of Meadow and another in front of Ian. "I'm basically serving you guys ketchup on cardboard. Not my style."

"It's the most delicious cardboard I ever tasted." Meadow shut down her musings, taking a huge bite from her square of pepperoni. She refused to wince when cheese scorched the roof of her mouth. She wouldn't give Rocco the pleasure.

"It's been so long since you ate lunch, you'd probably eat actual cardboard right now."

"Put enough peanut butter on it, and we'll see." Meadow shrugged and sipped fruit juice, letting it ease the burn before she swallowed. "Next time you're around, I'll have fresh tomatoes and herbs and whatever it is you need to make homemade gnocchi or sourdough bread or whatever." She poured on the sarcasm. "We all know you're the resident food hero."

"Don't you forget it." Rocco made a face at his pizza before he bit into it then washed it down with juice.

Ian watched with amusement as he chewed.

Probably he deserved an explanation. "Rocco was partially raised by his grandmother in Italy. He's the world's greatest chef, in case you were wondering."

"Second greatest. My grandma Luna is the tops." With a jerk of his chin, Rocco addressed Ian. "You hang around long enough, I'll make you a *salsa di pomodoro alla napoletana* that will change your life."

"He's not kidding." Just thinking about it made Meadow's mouth water, but she couldn't resist one more dig. "He really does think he can turn you into a different person with his superior cooking skills."

"'Superior cooking skills.'" Rocco mimicked her like a little brother needling his sister, his voice high-pitched and whiny, then looked at Ian and morphed into a professional. "So, the case we're working."

Ian nodded. "I'm all ears."

Debating how much she should say, Meadow put down her slice of pizza and dusted off her hands. "Ten years ago, three young men, late teens to early twenties, were killed on Valentine's Day. Their bodies were found in barns in Elk Valley, Wyoming."

"Mmm." Ian swallowed and swiped at his mouth with a napkin. "I remember that. They were all popped in the chest at point-blank range. The guys were all love-'em-and-leave-'em types, so the suspect pool was deep, and nobody was ever caught. They were all in some club together."

"You've done your homework." His jaw tight, Rocco tossed his napkin onto his plate, covering his pizza as though he'd lost his appetite. "The Young Ranchers Club. It was disbanded after the murders. The trail went cold, but nobody in Elk Valley has ever forgotten."

Meadow bit her lip. The case was personal to Rocco. He'd grown up in Elk Valley, and his father had investigated the murders, never giving up until he'd passed away a little over a year ago. Rocco had made it his personal mission to find the killer, and when new developments necessitated the formation of the Mountain Country K-9 Unit, he'd been one of the first deputized.

"Y'all are looking into that again?" Ian turned to Meadow. "Is this about the homicide you're investigating here that's linked to Elk Valley?"

"Yes." He'd remembered her comment in the bunker? *Impressive.* "Five months ago, on Valentine's Day, two bodies were found, one in Glacierville and one near Denver. Both shot in the chest with the same gun as the Elk Valley murders, and both found in barns. Both from Elk Valley. Both former members of the YRC."

"But this time there was a difference." Rocco shoved his plate aside and gripped the edges of the counter. "Only the Glacierville victim was a romancer. The other, Peter Windham, was a model citizen, great guy, professing Christian who walked the walk. The killer left notes on both of them. Typed, stabbed into their chests with a knife."

"The notes said, 'They got what they deserved. More to come across the Rockies. And I'm saving the best for last.'" The words chilled Meadow, especially since they'd already failed to save a sixth victim. "There was a third recent murder in Sagebrush, Idaho, a couple of months ago. Same MO, also a guy from Elk Valley's YRC."

Ian laid his napkin on his empty plate and slid it to the side, settling back to talk with a look in his eye that said he was ready to strategize. "Any link between the victims besides the YRC?"

"A dance." Rocco gathered the plates and stacked them. "All of them were at a dance about a month before the first killings. All of them but our good-guy victim participated in humiliating a young lady named Naomi."

"She a suspect?"

"She's been cleared." It had seemed to be a slam dunk, until Naomi's alibis checked out. "Even more concerning, the real killer is taunting us. He stole a therapy dog of ours, Cowgirl, and keeps making contact with our team leader, sending pictures, making vague threats. He's toying with us." Cowgirl was pregnant, which they knew from the killer's photos, and her puppies were due any day. The whole team was knotted up, watching the murderer use the dog to play mind games with them.

Rocco pounded the counter with his palm, rattling the

dishes. Both Meadow and Ian jumped. "It's sick. The sooner we catch him, the better." Jerking the plates from the counter, he headed for the sink and flicked the water on, his back to them.

Ian moved to speak, but Meadow laid a hand on his arm with a quick shake of her head. It was time to change the subject. Rocco needed a minute to deal with his personal feelings about the investigation. "I think the more pressing thing to worry about is that Silas and Des are still alive and how they found you."

"And what to do about Brooke." Ian stood and quickly filled in Rocco on the little he knew about his cousin's situation. "Whatever is going on, she's scared. I can't reach out to her with my phone busted. I never memorized her number." Something seemed to steal his next words. "I'm supposed to meet her first thing in the morning at the diner where she works, which means I'll need a vehicle."

"Des and Silas are looking for yours. We'll have it towed and put into storage so nothing happens to it."

"Same with yours, M. If they were watching it, they suspect it's connected to Ian. I can give you a ride." Rocco settled the last plate into the dish drainer, seeming to have calmed down. "Where does she work?"

Ian's gaze flicked between Meadow and Rocco as though he was making a decision.

She knew what it was because it was the same one she was coming to. They'd worked together before, knew how each other operated, had an unspoken language. "I've got it. I can run him into town to get a rental, and then we can both shadow him to the diner."

"Sounds like a plan." Drying his hands, Rocco called to Cocoa. "I think step one is we all get some rest. This day's gone on long enough."

She couldn't agree more. "Rocco, everything's set up as usual in the guest room. I've got a twin bed in the office, Ian." As tall as he was, his feet would likely hang out of the blankets most of the night, but he'd be okay.

After Rocco disappeared up the hallway and Meadow killed the lights, Ian followed her to his room with Grace at his heels. "No problem. It's light-years better than the bunker or the bushes."

Meadow flipped on the light as she walked into the room, then stepped aside and gestured as though the space was a grand hotel.

A twin bed, ready for guests, stood beneath a window on one wall. An L-shaped desk and two tall bookcases took up most of the remaining space.

Grace took a seat in the doorway, her head tilted. The K-9 knew it was bedtime, so she had to be wondering why they were in the office.

Ian looked down at her. "She's quite a partner. Very polite."

"Of course she is, but watch this." Meadow's eyes gleamed as she made eye contact with the K-9. "Grace, greet."

Immediately, Grace leaped up and pounced on Ian as though he was her new best friend. She licked his face and pawed at his chest.

Ian laughed, exactly as she'd hoped he would.

"Grace, down." The K-9 obediently sat at Meadow's side. Ian brushed off his shirt. "Awesome, but why?"

"It's a trick my mentor, Sully, taught me. I can use it to make her seem like a regular old dog, who's a little disobedient, if someone gets suspicious." She'd worked closely with Sullivan "Sully" Briggs back in the day, and he'd taught her several tips and tricks he'd picked up over the years. He was a well-respected K-9 officer with the US Marshals Service and had recently consulted on the RMK investigation.

Meadow swept her hand around the room, weariness cutting her amusement short. "You should be comfortable here. Breakfast is served when Rocco gets up and makes it." There wasn't anything in the fridge, but no doubt he'd be at the grocery story before dawn.

Ian walked to the desk and flicked the dried leaves of a potted plant near the window. "You keep a dead plant around?"

Meadow leaned against the doorframe. "That plant refuses to die. I watered it yesterday. In a day or so, it'll look like it was never neglected."

"If you say so."

"When my grandmother passed away, someone gave the plant to our family. Weirdly, no matter how long I forget about it, if I give it water, up it pops." She shrugged, slightly embarrassed. "It kind of makes me feel like she's still around, since it keeps coming back. I'll be sad if it ever officially kicks the bucket." It was silly, getting attached to a plant she rarely cared for, but it brought her comfort.

"I understand." Ian leaned against the desk. "Thanks for coming to the rescue today and for helping me out tomorrow. I know you're in the middle—"

From behind her closed bedroom door, something crashed. Glass shattered. The house alarm blared.

Meadow whirled toward the hall as Grace stood at attention, and Ian stepped up beside her, ready for battle.

SIX

There was no way Silas and Des had tracked them to Meadow's house…was there?

How?

Ian watched Meadow nod grimly to Rocco, who waited in the doorway of the guest room across the hall.

She texted something on her phone, then pocketed the device and spoke a quick command to Grace. The K-9 lay down under the desk but remained alert, watching Meadow. Without a word, she went to a safe on the bottom shelf of the nearest bookcase, opened it, and slipped a magazine into her Glock. She looked at him as she stood. "I know you're armed, but don't fire unless you have to. Stay here, as hard as that's going to be for you. I've reached out to Glacierville PD for backup."

Understood. Given that he wasn't officially in law enforcement, he could only act in self-defense.

He crouched near the door as she shut off the lights then stepped into the hall and whispered to Rocco before she moved toward her room.

Rocco went to the front of the house. After several beeps, the alarm shut off.

It took a moment for Ian's eyes to adjust. Light filtered through the blinds, likely from an outdoor light in the backyard.

The house was eerily silent, as though even the walls held their breath.

Ian exhaled slowly, his fingers tight around the pistol's grip. Since the shooting, he hated touching the thing, hated the memory of the last time he'd fired a weapon. While he carried it for protection, he hadn't pulled the trigger since that horrible day.

Meadow appeared in the doorway, a dim shadow in the milky light. "I'm going into my room. Rocco's got the living room and kitchen. Back me up."

This was risky. Anyone could be in her room. His heart hammered as he followed her to the bedroom door, taking up a position on one side as she pressed her back to the wall on the other.

With a quick nod, Meadow slowly turned the knob then pushed the door open, drawing back against the wall as though she expected bullets to fly.

Cold sweat broke out on Ian's skin.

There was only silence, so loud it almost deafened him.

Ian peeked around the doorframe. The bathroom light was on, and it illuminated the room. No one was inside. A window next to the bed was broken, but the hole wasn't large enough for a person to climb through.

The busted glass was either meant to draw them toward someone waiting outside to open fire when they appeared, or it was a diversion to distract them from the real attack.

"I've got movement at the back!" Rocco's shout from the kitchen was overlaid by a simultaneous gunshot and shattered glass.

Diversion.

Rocco's voice came again. "I'm fine. Shooter's taking potshots from the rear."

Meadow moved to run up the hall, but Ian sliced the air

with his hand to keep her in place. He slid along the wall into the guest room at an angle to her door then returned with a bed pillow, which he tossed into the air in front of her door.

A gunshot shattered the silence.

Ian and Meadow both jerked back against the wall.

Opening the door had given whoever was at the window a clear shot down the hallway.

They were trapped on either side of the door. Moving farther up the hall would put them straight into the shooter's line of sight. Ian was next to the guest room, but there was no way for Meadow to go anywhere without landing in the shooter's sights.

They were trapped, and Rocco was on his own.

His heart pounded. His head roared. Bullets were flying, and he could be hit. Meadow could be hit.

They were trapped.

Trapped.

Unless…

He looked across the hall at Meadow and kept his voice low. There was one way out, but it was all on him. "I can get out the guest room window." If he did, he would be in the front yard and could flank either the shooter at her window or the one toying with Rocco.

Assuming there were only two shooters…

The action might cost him everything. Could he physically force himself out the window when someone was firing on them?

Meadow stared at him, clearly evaluating his plan.

Come on, Meadow. Make it quick. There was no time to wait for backup to arrive, so they had to move, and the longer she waited, the more time his brain had to remember bullets were flying. Already, his muscles were threatening to give out.

Finally, she nodded. "Okay. But I'm praying. Hard."

He tightened his jaw. She could pray all she wanted. God wasn't concerned about Ian Carpenter.

Slipping into the guest room, Ian shut the door behind him to minimize any potential backlighting that might give away his position. He made his way to the window that faced the driveway and peered out from the side of the blinds.

One step at a time. One breath at a time. He could do this. He had to. Otherwise, they were trapped in a giant kill box.

It was also dark. The light from the backyard and the half-moon above cast shadows into the front yard, providing vague illumination.

Nothing seemed to be moving in front of the house, but there were too many places to hide. The trees offered cover. The vehicles offered cover. Des or Silas could move from position to position with little chance of being seen due to the deep shadows, and there was no guarantee only the two of them were lying in wait. There could be any number of potential attackers biding their time, waiting for a kill shot.

He could be gunned down before he even made it out the window.

He forced himself to breathe slowly. *One step at a time.*

Another shot cracked from the backyard, and Rocco fired back, the retort loud in the silence. "I've got one pinned behind the shed."

So they knew the position of one person out of a potentially limitless number of assailants.

Too many unknowns. Too many variables.

Yet they couldn't sit here waiting for a deadly assault. They had to be proactive.

Ian had to move.

One step at a time.

Every instinct said to curl into a ball beneath the window, yet Meadow's prayers must have been working because he somehow found the strength to keep moving. Standing to the side of the window, he wrapped the cord for the blinds around his fingers and slowly pulled.

His muscles tensed against a potential gunshot.

There was only silence.

Exposing his arm, he unlatched the window and raised it as gently as he could. It squeaked then moved easily, probably new windows from the obvious remodeling that had been done to the house.

Still no gunfire.

Either no one was watching or they were waiting for him to give them a clear shot.

A clear shot. His body went rigid. Ian pressed his spine to the wall and breathed in through his nose then out through his mouth. He rested his hand on the scar on his abdomen, phantom pain rushing through him. He could still feel the warmth of blood running between his fingers...could still see the flood of red.

The initial shot hadn't been the traumatic part. The aftermath had nearly done him in. The physical bullet to his body had been like a metaphorical bullet to his mind, leaving behind scars of vulnerability and anxiety he'd managed to wrestle to the ground...

Until today.

He exhaled through pursed lips. Meadow needed him. He was the only one in a position to save her and Rocco and their K-9 partners. Although he'd sincerely hoped never to be in a situation where a bullet could slam into him again, here he was. *Lord, help me.*

The prayer was unbidden, and with it came a fragment of scripture he'd heard at the rodeo chapel one Sunday. Something about God numbering his days and knowing what each of them would look like.

Even the day he was shot.

Even today.

God knew. Ian didn't. Was that comfort or not?

A few more deep breaths. A few more frantic prayers. Finally, his body agreed to move.

Braced for a shot, he stepped in front of the window. He slipped his right leg over the sill, holding his pistol tightly in his right hand as he steadied himself on the window frame with his left.

He had never been more vulnerable in his entire life. He hoped he'd never be this vulnerable again.

Something splintered the siding near his head. A gunshot cracked.

Fear rushed over him like a tsunami. He dove into the room and dropped beneath the window, his back to the wall. His ears roared. His heart pounded. His muscles turned to water.

Death was coming for him.

He couldn't do this.

"Ian! Status!"

Meadow's shout was a slap to his cheek. She was still trapped in the hall. He was still her only hope.

And he'd failed.

Wait. Instinct overrode fear. If the person who'd been waiting at Meadow's window was busy dealing with him, then… "Meadow! Move!" Hopefully she'd get the message that she was clear, at least for a few seconds.

A bullet hit the window, shattering glass that rained down on Ian.

Meadow's footsteps pounded up the hall. Her shadowed figure raced past the door, headed to help Rocco.

While Ian cowered.

"I've got the back. You take the front!" Rocco opened a barrage of fire.

"Got it!" Meadow responded.

Ian needed to cover Meadow, but fear rushed in, quickening his breath, robbing his muscles, scrambling his thoughts. He couldn't move. Couldn't think. Couldn't defend himself.

Couldn't protect anyone.

Sirens wailed in the distance, coming closer at a quick pace.

An unintelligible shout came from the backyard. In the woods by the house, something crashed through the brush, moving away.

Silas and Des were running instead of finishing the job of killing him.

He was too spent to pursue them. Shame burned his conscience. He'd failed.

From the rear of the house, Rocco's voice shouted, "Police! Stop and drop to your knees!"

Engines roared into the driveway, sirens blaring and lights reflecting off the walls.

On instinct, Ian slid the pistol across the floor away from him, sapping the last of his strength. There was no need to be mistaken for one of the bad guys and to come under friendly fire.

No, he had a feeling there was more fire about to rain down on him, and his back was covered in a huge, flashing target.

How had they been found?

Meadow slumped in a chair in the very Glacierville PD conference room she and Rocco had spent the previous day in. While it had been perfect for their investigative research, it had not functioned well as a place to bunk for the night. Sleep had been scarce; adrenaline and questions had chased her every time she closed her eyes. Silas and Des had managed to find her home, had known Ian was there. How? She couldn't solve that riddle. A whispered conversation with Rocco in the wee hours of the morning proved he had no answers either.

For a couple of hours, she'd managed to catnap on the floor under the table while Ian and Rocco tried to catch sleep in a couple of the chairs that lined the back wall of the room.

She'd slept under worse conditions, but after the relentless assault of the previous afternoon and evening, even a week in a luxury spa wouldn't provide enough rest.

It wasn't quite seven in the morning, and she was already tired of this room. Other than a quick outing with Grace a few minutes earlier, it felt like she'd spent her entire life hemmed in by these four beige walls. Somebody had better call with news soon, or she was liable to go out hunting the Thornton crew solo just to put an end to this Groundhog Day.

At her feet, Grace snorted and shifted, then settled back to sleep.

Meadow had never felt more jealous of another living creature in her life.

Since everyone had awakened starving for food, Ian had disappeared up the hall in search of a vending machine while Rocco had taken Cocoa outside for a short walk.

The night before, they'd opted to return to Glacierville for refuge at the PD while they plotted their next move. Meadow had exchanged several texts and calls with the leader of the Mountain Country K-9 Unit, Chase Rawlston, who was working to locate a safe house for them.

He couldn't find one soon enough.

Meadow had considered packing up the crew and heading back to Elk Valley, where the task force was headquartered, but it was fourteen hours away, and Ian would never leave without making contact with his cousin.

What she really wanted was her bed and some sleep, but her house was a crime scene, and with Des and Silas having evaded capture, her home was a no-go for the foreseeable future. There had to be a place where—

A pack of peanut-butter crackers landed on the table, dropped from above.

She looked up to find Ian standing behind her. "Breakfast is served. It was the best I could do on short notice. Turns out they don't serve omelets in vending machines."

"Ugh. I'll settle for peasant rations, then." She grinned as he sat a can of soda beside the crackers then rounded the table to sit across from her. It felt good to smile. It seemed like forever, which was roughly the length of this day, since she'd had a moment of levity.

It was also good to see Ian smile. He'd apologized repeatedly for "failing" her, but she'd argued each time. He'd drawn fire. Had cleared the way for her to move. That was bravery, not failure.

She opted to let that observation slide for the time being. "Chief Connor told me he'd try to bring in some hot chow with him, so we have something to look forward to."

"If I remember right, he's a fan of Clancy's, and they make a mean bacon, egg and cheese biscuit." Ian slid a pack of crackers and a drink toward the end of the table for Rocco, then tore the plastic from his own makeshift breakfast. "We're still in a holding pattern?"

"Until I hear back from our task force leader, yeah. He's got Glacierville PD and Cattle Bend PD and the Peak County sheriff on the hunt for the Thorntons and searching for a safe house for us. Hopefully, they'll come up with something soon. I reached out to my home office in Missoula, but we've got nothing right now. You know of anything?" This was Ian's old stomping grounds. He'd been a deputy for Peak

County before going undercover on the joint task force. It had been risky, but he was a guy who'd kept to himself and had few ties in the immediate area, so the undercover persona had worked.

Until Ronnie Thornton had Ian shot in retaliation.

Meadow used one finger to spin the orange crackers on the table. "I know it wasn't easy for you to put yourself in the line of fire tonight. Thanks." She couldn't help reassuring him again. She'd felt helpless, trapped in the hallway while Rocco and Ian put themselves in harm's way. Useless and helpless, two feelings she hated most. She didn't want Ian feeling that way.

Frankly, she'd also been terrified, especially when she'd heard the shot as Ian was leaving the house. She couldn't imagine his level of bravery, given that he knew what it felt like to have a bullet almost wipe him out of existence.

Ian picked up a cracker and studied it in the overhead light. "I don't want to talk about it anymore." He popped the cracker into his mouth and offered a dazzling smile that didn't reach his eyes. "So, which is better, cardboard pizza or vending machine crackers?"

He was trying to avoid his emotions. "Ian—"

"You're joking, right?" Rocco walked in and dropped into a chair at the head of the table as Cocoa settled at his feet. "Neither is real food, though I'm grateful to whichever one of you brought these in."

Meadow took a slow sip of soda, wishing Rocco had waited to return. She knew a deflection when she heard one, and Ian was a mirror bouncing his true emotions into space. If Rocco hadn't stepped in, she'd have called him on it. While she might take the liberty of digging deeper when it was just the two of them, she'd never risk embarrassing him in front of a fellow law enforcement officer.

Rocco cracked open his can of soda, took a long sip, then reached down and hefted his backpack off of the floor. "We have a video call in five minutes." He crammed an entire cracker into his mouth and started hooking up his laptop to the large monitor on the wall. Since they weren't working with classified evidence, they were allowed to use their own electronics in the building.

With all that had happened, she'd almost forgotten about the call. Chase liked to check in with the team every other day, but yesterday afternoon he'd texted about a mandatory all-hands meeting. Maybe there had been a break in their murder investigation.

She hoped so. While she loved her teammates, she was tired of running the roads between here and Elk Valley.

Ian stood and drained his can of soda. "I'm going to step out and see if the chief is here. Maybe he'll have a bag of those biscuits." He left the room, shutting the door behind him.

Smart man. He knew the call would include classified intel, and he hadn't waited to be kicked out.

They logged on and, as soon as they appeared on the screen, team leader Chase Rawlston acknowledged their presence. "We're waiting on Isla. She had a tech issue."

There were a few tired chuckles. Ironic, since Isla Jiminez was their technical expert.

The team looked as exhausted as Meadow felt. The serial homicides were taking a toll, especially on members like Rocco, Chase and rookie Ashley Hanson, who were from Elk Valley and had a vested interest in the case. When the serial killer had popped up again ten years after the first three murders, the FBI had called Chase in to lead the Mountain Country K-9 Unit. As the Wyoming Bureau supervisory special agent, he was familiar with the area and with the investigation.

Isla appeared on the screen, her brown hair pulled back in a ponytail. "Sorry, guys. I let my laptop battery die."

Detective Bennett Ford laughed. "Now I've heard it all."

"Yeah," Deputy Selena Smith chimed in. "You can't harass us when we make technical errors from now on."

"As amusing as this is," Chase cut off the banter, "we've got some details to discuss. With Meadow and Rocco caught up in the middle of an assassination attempt on a witness fresh out of WITSEC who's now under attack again, we've all got better things to do than to chat our time away on here."

Nobody said a word. They'd already received texts about the goings-on with Meadow and Rocco, and several had reached out. Because they were all tied up in their own investigations, they couldn't offer much more than moral support.

Isla took over the conversation. "I'm the one who asked for this meeting. I've got an update on Cowgirl and a possible lead on our killer."

Cowgirl, a therapy dog meant to help comfort victims and witnesses, had been gifted to the unit by Ashley's father. Within days, the K-9 had been dognapped from their HQ in Elk Valley—and the team had come to believe that the thief was the Rocky Mountain Killer. One of the photos that the RMK had taunted them with featured the labradoodle wearing a pink dog collar with the word *Killer* spelled out in rhinestones.

It was sick.

"Is she okay?" Ashley leaned closer to her camera. "I hate to think of her out there in this guy's hands. I mean, I know he seems to be taking care of her, but with her puppies due any day, what will he do to her? What's his endgame?"

They were all questions the team had wrestled with since Cowgirl had vanished.

For weeks, Isla had been trying to track down where the

collar had come from. She'd learned little beyond the fact that it was a common item sold in gift shops along the Rockies, including in Sagebrush, Idaho, where a tip had been called in that Cowgirl had been spotted. Her pregnancy and the unique brown spot on her ear made her easy to identify, and they'd blanketed social media with descriptions, hoping for a hit.

"Late yesterday, I may have landed on something during a phone call with a boutique owner in Sagebrush. When I sent her photos of Cowgirl, she remembered her because of the markings on her ear and because it's rare to see a labra-doodle as obviously pregnant as she is out and about. The owner said a tall, good-looking blond man bought the collar. He had on a hat and sunglasses, and she was more focused on the dog than on the man."

"Can we trace a credit card?" FBI Agent Kyle West hopped into the conversation.

"He paid cash. That also stood out to her since most of her customers are tourists who tend to pay with cards."

There was a collective sigh of disappointment.

"Oh, but wait," Isla singsonged. "I'm not done. He stood out also because he had an unusual tattoo on his forearm. A knife."

It wasn't a lot, but it was something. At this point, every little bit helped.

"I've made sure that was added to our BOLO." Chase took control of the meeting. "We've updated the website and so-cial media, also. Now, before we log off, I want to see what we can do for Meadow and Rocco while—"

"Chase?" Bennett Ford raised his hand as though he was in school. He looked grim, as though someone had delivered bad news. "I think we might have a problem."

SEVEN

Meadow leaned forward, and her toe tapped Grace's belly under the table. The K-9 stirred and rose, moving to stand beside Meadow with her head resting on her partner's thigh, watching intently for a command.

Absently, Meadow scratched Grace's ears, her eyes on the screen. Bennett had recently married Naomi Carr-Cavanaugh, their initial suspect in the murders. A month prior to the first killings ten years earlier, Naomi had been taunted by several bullies at a dance hosted by the Young Ranchers Club. Naomi had been a bit of a wallflower, but she'd accepted an invite to the dance from Trevor Gage, one of the more popular young men in the group. When she'd arrived, Trevor's friends had pounced, telling Naomi that Trevor considered her a joke and had only invited her to get her hopes up. She'd fled, devastated by their cruelty, and Trevor had left the dance not long after.

A month later, on Valentine's Day, the first three victims had been murdered. Seth Jenkins, Brad Kingsley and Aaron Anderson were lured to a barn via text messages sent from a burner phone: Meet me at YRC barn at midnight followed by a kiss emoji. The guys were known to be serial daters and dumpers, so there were a lot of suspects who might want revenge.

Including Naomi, who had every reason to use a romantic holiday to wreak vengeance on the young men who had humiliated her.

But when the unit investigated Naomi, then recently widowed and heavily pregnant, her alibis for all of the murders cleared her, including the three most recent ones. Additionally, the Colorado victim, Peter Windham, had been a friend of hers, leaving her with no motive for his killing.

Bennett's statement raised the level of concern for everyone on the team, though. He and Naomi had connected during the investigation when she was targeted by an unrelated killer. They'd married recently, and if he saw a problem, it was possible he'd learned new information about his wife.

Meadow prayed it wasn't so. They were so happy together. To think Bennett might suspect Naomi of—

"What are you saying, Bennett?" FBI Agent Kyle West spoke first, echoed by the mumbles of other members of the team. "Is Naomi okay?"

"She's fine. The baby's fine. The three of us are fine." The baby had been born shortly before their wedding. "It's more that I feel I should bring up, well, my brother-in-law."

"Evan?" It seemed unlikely Evan Carr was their killer. The original investigators had followed that road before, as had their unit, and they'd come up empty both times. "He had a solid alibi for the first set of murders." Evan had been with his girlfriend, Pauline Potter, that night, and she'd confirmed that.

"I don't know." Their rookie officer, Ashley Hanson, looked a bit uncomfortable in the spotlight. "I interviewed Evan a few months ago because his sister was a suspect. He was genuinely concerned about the murders and empathetic, aware of the pain the deaths had caused everyone. Elk Valley isn't that big. Everyone knows each other. And Evan wasn't even a part of the Young Ranchers Club. He ran with a different crowd. The YRC was Naomi's thing, and I don't know that they were close enough for him to seek vengeance on her behalf, not in such a violent manner, anyway."

Chase took the reins again. "Bennett, what makes you leery now?"

"I don't know." Bennett dragged his hand down his face as he leaned back in his chair, away from his laptop's camera. "I just want to stay above board and to be sure we've checked all of the boxes. In all fairness, he's a tall, good-looking blond guy, like the boutique owner said."

"So are you, Bennett." Rocco's comment was met with a few chuckles. "It's not exactly a unique description."

"No, but among our suspect pool who were around at the time and might have even the slightest motive, it's worth sending the boutique owner a photo just to rule him out conclusively. And honestly? Sometimes it feels like there's something I just can't put my finger on." Bennett sat forward. "I'm just trying to think the way I'd think if he wasn't my brother-in-law. When we finally arrest a suspect, I don't want a lawyer to point at us and say we might have played favorites. It might be time to interview Evan again, simply to take him completely off the list."

"I get it." Chase tapped something on his keyboard. "You have a photo? We'll have Isla reach out to the boutique owner with it. The guy was wearing sunglasses, but it's still worth a shot."

Picking up his phone, Bennett scrolled on the screen. "I've got a couple of photos." He held the phone up to the camera, revealing the image of a handsome young man with short blond hair.

"Send that one to Isla." Chase said. "There are a million other tall blond guys in the world, but you're right, he's close to the investigation and we need to make sure our ducks are in a row. You know where he is right now?"

"He travels a lot, so it's probable he's on-site with his recruiting company. I can check."

"He have a tattoo?"

"Not that I know of. And since he and Naomi have never been close and haven't spent any time together recently, I doubt she'd know, but I'll ask her. He's been so busy that he's been by only once to see the baby, and that was a brief visit."

"From what I've heard about Evan, he's not the kind of guy to get inked," Rocco said. He'd know, having grown up in Elk Valley. Ashley nodded in agreement. While Evan had been several grades ahead of Rocco and Ashley, they all would have crossed paths in town. "He has a reputation for being business-focused and kind of straitlaced. A visible tat would be completely out of character. If I can, I'd like to get in on that interview, though."

"No." Chase shook his head. "I need you to stick with Meadow, and I think I want someone who doesn't know him to chat with him this time. I want a totally objective, clean-slate viewpoint so we can avoid future questions about bias."

Rocco nodded grimly. "Understood."

There was an uncomfortable silence. Chase rarely denied their requests.

Isla cleared her throat and looked into the camera. "In the meantime, I'll also put together a list of tall blond men who were members of the YRC or who were at the dance that night."

"Might want to expand that to the entire high school." Standing, Rocco looked at the camera. "Everyone knew what happened. And while Naomi sort of kept to herself, there were still some people who were pretty upset that anyone could be as mean as those guys were. Also, given their reputations for loving 'em and leaving 'em, we can't forget we could also be looking at a jealous boyfriend. This might not be about Naomi at all."

"That's right." Looking to the right, Chase appeared to listen to someone off camera. He nodded then turned back to the group. "Let's not get tunnel vision. I know it's difficult. We've got six dead and a threat to an unknown seventh. We can't afford to make a mistake. And, Meadow?"

"Yes?" A buzz ran through her as though she'd just been called to the principal's office. Getting called out by name in meetings wasn't something she was used to.

"You and Rocco stay on the line. I've got some resources for you."

A chorus of goodbyes bounced from the speakers, and one by one, the other members of the team disappeared until only Chase was left. "I've got a lead on a place for you to lie low, but you may want to recon it first. I'm going to text it to you. Keep in mind, my hands are tied in some respects, but I'll do what I can. I've talked to the local authorities and gotten you and Rocco clearance to help out with this, but you don't have full capability. The FBI isn't ready to jump in yet without more proof, so we aren't officially involved, but Isla is available to consult."

"Understood." Meadow glanced over her shoulder at the closed door then stepped closer to the screen on the wall and the microphone it contained. "Ian Carpenter believes his cousin is in trouble or in proximity to trouble based on a series of texts she's sent him. He's set up a meet with her this morning in Cattle Bend. I think we should be there."

"It puts you out in the open in a town where he's already been hunted."

"Hiding at my house didn't help him." She exhaled loudly. "I'd like to know how that happened."

"I'll see what we can do." Chase wrote something on a paper by his hand. "As far as taking Ian out in public, I'm unsure."

When she looked at Rocco, he nodded grimly as he stepped up beside her. "We have no hold on him. He'll go on his own if we don't back him up, and that's not wise. He's a former law enforcement officer, and he's worked with Meadow before. We can't let a brother go in without covering him."

"No, you can't. If something were to happen to him neither of you would ever be able to wash his blood off your hands." With a tight expression, Chase gave a quick nod. "Do what you need to, but be careful, and I'll chat with the higher-ups and try to get you tapped into more of our resources. Keep me updated."

"Thanks, Chase." Meadow killed the call and turned to Rocco. "You don't have to get involved. You can stay here in Glacierville and keep digging into Henry Mulder's murder, keep yourself out of the line of fire." There was no way he'd do that. Lying back when there was action happening wasn't like Rocco at all.

He grinned. "You know me better than that." As he unhooked the laptop from the big screen, he sobered. "You realize this whole thing is foolish, right? The best thing for Ian to do is to let us go in and see if we can find his cousin. Your bad guys might know who we are, but we're going to be a lot less recognizable to them than he is, at least at first sight."

"True." Maybe that was the thing to do. If they borrowed an unmarked car from Glacierville PD, maybe they could roll in and reach out to Ian's cousin on his behalf without exposing him to a potentially deadly encounter.

Meadow headed for the door with Grace close behind, prepared to call Ian back inside. Rocco's plan was solid.

The problem would be convincing Ian not to put himself in the line of fire.

* * *

The closer they got to Cattle Bend, the more Ian regretted agreeing to Rocco and Meadow's plan. In the back seat of an SUV with darkly tinted windows, he drummed his fingers on his knee and watched the world pass by. The vehicle they'd borrowed from the impound at Glacierville PD smelled of stale cigarette smoke and beer. When it came to the stains on the seats, he didn't care to hazard a guess.

None of that bothered him though. He'd been in a lot worse places, and he had bigger problems. He'd failed Meadow in a gunfight. Had folded under pressure.

Was he about to fail Brooke as well?

With his phone busted, he couldn't reach out to his cousin to tell her he was on the way. A few minutes earlier, in an effort to calm Ian's nerves, Meadow had called the diner to make sure Brooke was safely at work.

No one had answered any of the five times she'd dialed.

Ian's gut screamed something had gone wrong.

Meadow caught his eye in the rearview. She'd pulled her hair into a ponytail and was wearing a borrowed baseball cap and her sunglasses. "You okay back there?" She'd been quiet for most of the hour-long drive.

Rocco had been silent as well, but that was because he'd fallen asleep almost as soon as they hit the road. Law enforcement officers and soldiers could sleep anywhere, that was for sure.

Still, the silence in the car was weighted with everyone's physical and emotional exhaustion.

Exhaustion he'd foisted upon them when he'd dragged them into his chaos. The more he thought about it, the more he believed he could have saved himself in the forest. Instead, he'd panicked and called for backup. Now Meadow and her team were in the crosshairs, whether Ian liked it or not. Telling her to back off would never work. That was one thing he'd learned from experience.

"Ian?"

He might as well answer. Her persistence was legendary. "A lot is running through my mind."

"Well, one of those things had better not be regret for reaching out to me yesterday." She flicked a gaze into the rearview. "I'd be pretty upset if you were out there trying to fix this on your own."

"I don't doubt it." He tapped his knee, wishing she'd try to call the diner again. "Why wouldn't a business answer their phone?"

"Maybe it's the breakfast rush."

Maybe. It was nearing nine, and Cattle Bend was a rising tourist town, so it was possible. "It worries me since Brooke was so cagey about something being wrong. I don't like it." Especially not with a target on his back. Brooke had been convinced one of her close friends was talking to a predator online, and she'd reached out to Ian. Since she was the one person who seemed to care about him, Ian would move mountains to help her.

And, sure, maybe he'd been looking for an excuse to come back. Maybe he'd hoped to run into Meadow. Maybe—

"You don't think she's somehow landed on Silas's radar, do you?"

That thought had barreled through his brain sometime in the middle of last night, when he'd been too keyed up with adrenaline to fall asleep. "I'd like to think not. My family isn't close. Brooke is my mom's sister's kid, so she doesn't share my last name. I haven't been around her in a couple of years and only established contact again after Ronnie died. We text and email and talk on the phone. No letters to intercept. They'd have to be pretty astute to figure out there's a connection between us, but you never know. Silas is smarter than he looks."

"You're probably right." Meadow navigated the exit to Cattle Bend, coasting to a stop at the top of the off-ramp, where a red light shined. "If they had any clue Brooke was related to you, they'd have used that intel to draw you out last night."

True. "I don't think they were aware I was in town until they spotted me in Cattle Bend yesterday. I'd just parked in front of the diner and was about to head inside when they basically charged me with their vehicle. If they made their way back there and started asking questions…" Then the worst might have happened. If they started nosing around and connected Brooke to him, then she'd be in danger.

He should have told Brooke to lie low, but her number wasn't one he'd memorized. Her mother's house phone was disconnected, likely because they'd all moved to cell service. He had no clue how to reach out to his family without simply showing up on their doorstep. He hadn't spoken to most of them in fourteen years, not since Dean had died. When his cousin wrapped his car around a tree after a party, it had been the final cut that severed Ian from his family. Everyone had laid the blame at Ian's feet.

Everyone except Brooke. Even as a kid, she'd recognized her brother's partying ways and stubborn arrogance. Yes, Ian had been at the party with his cousin. No, he hadn't been drinking, although Dean had downed half the liquor cabinet along with who knew what else.

Ian had taken his cousin's keys, but he hadn't counted on Dean having the spare in his pocket.

Brooke had lost her brother that night, and she'd looked to Ian to fill the void.

Now, she might be in trouble, and he was failing her. "What if she's been trying to reach me? What if something—"

"We've got someone getting you a new phone so you won't have to go into a store and risk putting yourself in the open for too long. And you'll feel a lot better once Rocco and I get into that diner and lay eyes on your cousin. We can prove to you she's okay and set up a meet so the two of you can talk somewhere safe."

Assuming they weren't spotted by Silas or a lookout.

Dropping his head on the back of the seat, Ian closed his eyes. Since when was he such a pessimist?

His hand went to his abdomen. Since he took a bullet in a parking lot where he should have been safe. The world would have to forgive him if he didn't trust any promise that said things were going to turn out fine.

When the light turned green, Meadow didn't release the brake.

From the right, a siren wailed as a Cattle Bend police cruiser slowed at the intersection then rushed through.

Ian watched it speed up the road and around a curve. There was an adrenaline rush to law enforcement work that he didn't often feel anymore. It wasn't a high, but a feeling of heading into the fray, being the one to help. Although he was happy with his quiet life with the horses at the rodeo, the protector instinct still called to him.

Meadow eased off of the brake and made the turn toward downtown. "You don't talk about your family much. Do—"

"We there yet?" Rocco shifted and stretched, his voice thick with sleep.

Saved by the groggy bell. His family was the last thing he wanted to discuss with Meadow.

She pursed her lips, then her demeanor shifted. "You're worse than my five-year-old niece, Roc."

"So when I start whining about how I want a burger from the drive-through and the little toy that comes with it, you won't be surprised." He stretched, pressing his palms against the ceiling, then looked over his shoulder at Ian. "Is the coffee any good at this diner where your cousin works?"

"Never been there. It's fairly new. Guy who used to run the kitchen at one of the ski resorts opened it up a couple of years ago, and it got popular pretty quickly." At least according to Brooke. She'd told him a while back that tips were good. "It's on the north end of the main road, on the right. When we set up a time to meet, she said we'd have to park in the back because they've eliminated street parking. Cattle Bend is getting more tourists since they revitalized the downtown."

Having seen the money coming in from travelers who were looking for the old-fashioned Western town experience, Cattle Bend had built facades and worked to attract independent business owners and restaurateurs to the area. He'd hardly recognized the place when he'd arrived yesterday. They'd really changed so—

"Uh-oh." Rocco lowered his arms and leaned closer to the windshield.

Dread pooled in Ian's stomach as Meadow inhaled deeply and gripped the steering wheel with both hands.

Ian forced himself to look out the front window as the main street through downtown came into view.

Three police cars blocked the road on the north end. A fire truck and an ambulance were also on scene…

Parked directly in front of the diner.

EIGHT

Meadow pulled in behind one of the police cars, her intuition running on overdrive.

This was about to be very bad for Ian.

Rocco was out the SUV and holding his identification up to an approaching officer before Meadow could kill the ignition.

She unbuckled her seat belt and turned to Ian. "Stay in the vehicle."

"No way I'm—"

"Stay. In. The. Vehicle." Her voice was hard, the one she used on suspects who weren't cooperating. "Use your head. If this is about Brooke, then it's likely Silas, Des or someone working for them who is keeping an eye out for you. Stay low. Don't move unless Rocco or I come for you. No arguments." She pegged him with her sternest gaze. "Tell me you understand and you'll do it, because I'd hate to pull that whole TV cop thing and handcuff you to the steering wheel."

The vague attempt at humor didn't land. Ian stared at her for so long she was certain he was going to buck. Finally, he huffed a loud breath. "Fine. I get it."

She laid a hand on his knee. There had to be a way to ease his pain, which tugged at her heart. "I know you want to go in with a full head of steam to make sure Brooke is okay. This may not be about her at all. Just hold still until we know. I don't need you getting hurt." The day he'd been shot had gutted her, and she still had nightmares about it. She certainly never wanted to relive it. Believing she was close to losing someone who'd come to mean so much—

No.

Meadow shoved the emotions aside. Whatever was happening in the diner needed her full attention. Any past or present feelings for Ian could wait in the back seat with him.

When she joined Rocco at the rear of the SUV, they leashed Cocoa and Grace then headed for the perimeter, where emergency personnel moved between vehicles and the building with a frightening sense of urgency.

Bringing the dogs would blow their attempt to lie low, but they rarely left their K-9 partners behind. She scanned the area, searching for anyone watching too closely. Red, white and blue lights from first responders' vehicles flashed off of buildings and faces. Among the crowd of about twenty who had gathered, no one seemed overly interested in them, and no one was watching their SUV.

They showed their credentials to the Cattle Bend police officer standing guard, then Meadow hung her badge around her neck as she slipped under the tape with Rocco close behind. They were in civilian clothes, having hoped to keep anyone who might be a threat from immediately recognizing them. That hope was gone.

Inside the diner, chaos had left its mark. Several tables were overturned, their chairs flung onto their sides. Behind the counter, the jagged edges of a large shattered mirror clung to the teal-colored wall, while shards of glass were scattered across the counter and floor.

Rocco shot her a worried look.

"Deputy Marshal Ames." At the familiar voice, Meadow

turned and found Cattle Bend Police Chief Gloria Montgomery striding toward them. The woman was tall with posture that made Meadow envious. She walked with the grace of a supermodel. Her blond hair was in a low bun on her neck, and the polished look only added severity to her grim expression.

Chief Montgomery nodded to Rocco but addressed Meadow. "What brings you to our crime scene?" It was a friendly question, a curiosity, not a challenge.

"Honestly, I wasn't aware I would be walking into a crime scene." Meadow didn't want to leak too much of Ian's story, since they needed to lie low, but she also didn't want to be evasive. "I'm here on unofficial business, looking for a friend who's a waitress. Brooke Hawlett."

Chief Montgomery's mouth opened, then closed. Her expression tightened as she glanced at Rocco before meeting Meadow's gaze again. "You're sure this is unofficial?"

Rocco's posture tightened, but he said nothing. He'd heard the odd undertone to the question as well.

Likely, he sensed the same tension Meadow did. "Chief, are we stepping into something we should know about?"

"What's your business with Brooke Hawlett?" Where there had been a friendly, open expression moments before, a shadow now crossed the chief's face.

It took everything in Meadow not to buck at the question. This was Cattle Bend's crime scene, and it was their territory. She enjoyed a friendly relationship with all of the law enforcement in the area, and she didn't want to jeopardize that by popping off over a simple question. But she felt stonewalled, as though the chief who was usually so forthcoming was withholding information or stalling with her answers.

Meadow wanted to get to Brooke then get moving so Ian was out of harm's way, but as she surveyed the room and measured her words, she saw no one who matched the photos he had shown her.

Where was Ian's cousin?

Taking a deep breath, Meadow forced her voice to remain even. "All I can say is I have a friend who's worried about her. This person believes Brooke may be in trouble and wants to be sure she's safe. This is more of a…courtesy wellness check." As much as she wanted to step closer and crowd the chief's personal space, Meadow held her spot. "Is she safe?"

"What made this person assume Brooke might be in trouble?"

Okay, enough was enough. Ian had been in the car too long. They were standing in the middle of a crime scene.

And there was no way to know who was watching.

It was clear Brooke had been involved in whatever incident had destroyed the diner and brought the police onto the scene.

"With all due respect, Chief, I'm on a time crunch. I've got a dangerous situation that's evolving rapidly, and I need to talk to Brooke Hawlett as soon as possible. I'm asking for some leeway here."

"And I'm trying to solve a kidnapping."

Rocco muttered something under his breath as Meadow took an involuntary step back at the force of what wasn't spoken. "Someone took Brooke?"

"Pretty violently." The chief gave a curt nod and seemed to come to a decision. "Two masked assailants pulled up to the front door about fifteen minutes ago, shot up the place and grabbed Brooke. She fought every inch of the way, but…" The chief gestured toward the overturned tables. "It was over in under a minute. We've got a BOLO out for a dark four-door sedan headed south out of town. So far, no hits."

Meadow balled her fist around Grace's leash. They were

too late. There was almost zero doubt Silas or someone working for him had taken Brooke.

But had Silas targeted Brooke for trafficking? Or was this an attempt to draw Ian out of hiding? Given the very public nature of the snatch and grab, it was likely about Ian, which meant the danger increased the longer he was in public. "What else have you got?"

"We've just started talking to witnesses, and I've got one of my guys viewing security-camera footage, but it seems they headed directly for Brooke as though she was the target." Chief Montgomery stepped closer and lowered her voice. "Maybe you've heard or maybe not, but we've had several young people vanish in the past four months. All around Brooke's age, but the others weren't taken like this. A couple were lured by an online predator. One was homeless and frequented a travel plaza near the interstate. One disappeared from a party where there was a steady flow of alcohol and drugs. Up until today, I thought we might have a serial killer on our hands, and when I saw you walk in with your federal agent self, I pretty much decided my theory was right."

"You were wrong. We're not dealing with a serial killer." Rocco spoke for the first time. His expression tight, he looked to Meadow for confirmation it was time to share what they knew. When she nodded, he turned to the chief. "Silas Thornton has been spotted in the area."

Chief Montgomery held up her index finger, her head tilted as though she was trying to process the information. She almost spoke, then she pointed to Rocco as though she was having to wade through shock. "Silas Thornton is long gone. The scourge of that family was burned off when he died in an explosion and his father died in prison. It took years and a joint operation to shut them down. Silas is not back in action."

"I don't blame you for wanting it to be a mistake." The Thorntons had robbed the outlying towns around the city of Missoula of any sense of safety and security. They'd trafficked countless young women and men through the area, holding them in warehouses and other spaces scattered around Missoula. Occasionally, they'd hunted in the region, picking off vulnerable teenagers. Though they typically sought runaways, they sometimes lured other victims as well. There had been a collective sigh of relief when the organization was torn apart. To think they were active again in the same location was unimaginable.

"What proof do you have?"

"A reliable witness has laid eyes on them. I've heard their voices and enough of their own words to believe it's them."

"Them?" Chief Montgomery's eyebrows knit together. "Who's with him?"

"Desiree Phelps."

"Wow." The chief puffed out the exclamation. "The team is alive and well and working again."

"And out for blood. They've attacked a witness, and last night, they made a run at the same person when he sought protection at my house."

"That was you last night? I heard about the call for Glacierville PD and Peak County, but I hadn't been briefed on any details."

There was no time to offer them now. They needed to get moving. The longer they stood around talking, the larger Silas's head start grew. "We're working with a unit investigating the Rocky Mountain Killer, but we have some leeway on other cases as well. I'm going to call my team leader and see if we can officially assist." Given the violence of the crime and their suspicions, it might be enough to get the feds involved.

Chief Montgomery nodded. "I have a feeling I'm going to want you guys here. Let's shut this down before it goes too far."

And before Brooke was killed.

What was taking so long?

Each sweep of the second hand on his watch took hours. Every one of the ten minutes since Meadow and Rocco had disappeared inside the diner had hit him like a body blow.

Was Brooke hurt? Why hadn't Meadow stepped out with an update?

Ian reached for the door then let his hand drop to the stained upholstery. As much as he wanted to rush in and save the day, he could land them all in hot water if he showed his face. For all he knew, Silas and Des had created a commotion simply to draw him out. There could be a sniper on a rooftop, an assailant with a knife in the crowd...

Without knowing who, if anyone, Silas had on his payroll, there were too many unknowns. Anyone could be a killer.

He hadn't felt this helpless since he'd awakened in the hospital attached to so many tubes and wires that his initial foggy thoughts had made him believe he was hooked up to the Matrix. Ever since that day, he'd controlled every situation.

The past sixteen hours had proven control was an illusion. There was nothing he could do to manage the increasing chaos surrounding him. The longer he sat, the more convinced he was Brooke was in danger, but if he left the vehicle...

He could relive the feeling of a bullet slamming into him, only this time, the lead might finish its job.

His jaw clenched. Was this what he'd been reduced to? He'd once taken an oath to protect and serve; now he was bowing to fear instead of helping the one person in his life who'd never turned her back on him.

Ian shoved the car door open, stepped out and charged up the street. He ducked under the police tape and headed for the diner's open door like he belonged there.

He almost made it.

Two officers flanked him before he could cross the threshold.

The one to the right stepped into the doorway, while the one to the left took up a position beside him. "Sir, I'm going to need to see some identification."

The guy wanted a badge, something Ian hadn't carried in two years. While he wanted to charge forward, he didn't want the handcuffs that would follow. Inhaling deeply, he held his hands away from his body to indicate he was no threat. "I have a driver's license in my wallet in my back pocket, but I don't have my badge." *Or any badge at the moment.* "I'm with the deputy marshal who's inside, Meadow Ames."

The cop blocking his way raised an eyebrow. His blue eyes held a heavy dose of skepticism and wariness, a look Ian himself had worn on more occasions than he cared to count. "I suggest you go back to your vehicle. This is an active crime scene."

An active crime scene where his younger cousin worked. Ian wanted to shove past the guy and call out for Brooke. Instead, he scanned the interior of the diner, finally spotting Rocco and Meadow near the counter at the rear. "Meadow!" Her name echoed off the walls.

She turned quickly, her ponytail swinging, and her expression morphed from curiosity to anger.

Yeah, he'd pay for not following orders, but he'd deal with that later. "Tell them to let me in."

He'd read about people whose anger looked like a thundercloud on their faces before, but he'd never seen it until now. If a face really could storm, it was highly likely he'd have already been struck by lightning.

She stopped behind the officer at the door. "I ought to have them arrest you. You'd be safer from yourself behind bars." When the officer moved his hand to his hip, she shook her head. "No. He's with me and Officer Manelli. You can let him in."

With a curt nod, the two officers stood down.

Before Ian could move, Meadow grabbed him by the wrist and dragged him to a wide wall between the two front windows. "Have you lost your mind?" The words barely made it through her gritted teeth.

The last thing he was worried about was Meadow's ire. "Where's Brooke?"

He tried to step around Meadow, but her palm against his chest shoved him against the wall. "Ian, stay away from the windows. If you can handle that, I'll bring the manager over, and we can talk about what's going on." The pressure on his sternum increased. "Are we clear this time?"

"Crystal." The humiliation of being talked down to burned the back of his neck. She might have been his handler on that op, but she didn't get to boss him around now.

Except…she was right about staying away from the windows. His shoulders lost some of their defiance. "Where is she?"

The pressure on his chest decreased, but Meadow didn't move her hand. Instead, her fingers curled as though she could wrap his heart against her palm to protect it from whatever happened next.

Well, she didn't need to protect him. "This mess in here… Someone took Brooke. By force." He was going to be sick.

Meadow swallowed hard. "If it helps, she fought them all the way."

He looked away, staring at the remains of a shattered mirror behind the counter. Brooke had lived a hard life with con-artist parents who had been neglectful before Dean died and who had canonized her brother after, constantly ignoring her in their grief and anger. That she was a fighter didn't surprise him, but such a trait could either save her life or get her killed.

Meadow's fingers tightened against his chest, her palm warm and her touch somehow soothing.

When Ian turned his head, she was watching him as though she wanted to speak, but then she simply dropped her hand and motioned for Rocco to join them.

He crossed the diner, stepping around an overturned table, followed by a man who picked his way across the room to avoid stepping on the debris that littered the tile floor.

For the first time, the trail of destruction came into focus. The broken mirror, the scattered tables and chairs… Brooke truly had done all she could to save herself, but someone had clearly come in with a mission.

He had a horrible feeling he knew who it was.

The manager, a middle-aged man with dark hair that had begun to gray around the temples, gathered in the huddle with Meadow and Rocco. His face was pale from what had clearly been a traumatic experience.

Meadow took the lead. "Mr. Pullman, this is Ian Carpenter. He's—"

"Brooke's cousin." The manager's expression collapsed. "I'm so sorry—"

"How did you know that?" Ian's chest squeezed. Nobody should know his name, let alone his relationship to Brooke. "Who told you?"

"I…" Mr. Pullman's head jerked back as though Ian had slapped him. He looked to Rocco as though seeking permission to speak and received a terse nod. "She…she mentioned you a couple of days ago. Said she had a cousin who used to be a deputy and she was worried about one of her friends who was talking to a guy online. She thought it sounded suspicious, but her friend wasn't listening and neither was her mom, so she'd reached out to him."

Ian sagged against the wall as his stomach crashed to his feet. After Ronnie Thornton died in prison, Ian had planned to stay in his new life in Texas. When he'd reached out to Brooke to let her know he was safe and they could resume contact, he'd asked her not to talk to the family about him. He hadn't thought there was a need to caution her about mentioning his name in public. "Did anyone overhear her? Ask her about me?"

Pullman's eyes shifted sideways, as though he didn't want to say what he remembered.

Ian felt like shaking him. Did this man not understand the urgency? Forcing himself to remain calm, he balled his fists instead.

"Anything will help." Meadow's voice was more gentle than Ian's would have been.

"I guess you'd told her you were coming into town, and early this morning, she was pretty excited. She was talking to me and to a couple of her regular customers about it."

"Who were those regulars? And were there any strangers around when she was talking?" Surely Silas and Des weren't hanging around town on the regular, but they could have dropped into the diner while they were scouting locations, or they could have been the online boyfriend Brooke was concerned about and had been in town to work one of their heinous plans.

"I can make you a list, but none of them would do what those thugs today did to Brooke. It was mostly the old-timers in here when she was talking. But... I mean, there are always tourists around, so yeah, there were a few strangers, too."

"One of the Cattle Bend officers is in the back, running through the security video." Rocco was already backing away. "I'll go have him dial back to yesterday, see if they see her talking to anyone else or if there's anyone we recognize on the feed."

"Anyone you recognize?" Pullman straightened, his expression hard. "Is there a reason a federal agent is here? What do we not know? What *should* we know?" His voice was rising as his shock and fear morphed into doubts and anger. "Are our kids in danger again? We just went through this with—"

"Mr. Pullman." Meadow laid a hand on the man's shoulder, and he instantly quieted at her voice, which was somehow both authoritative and soothing. Even Ian couldn't help responding to it. "All we have right now is speculation, and we can't make official comments based on speculation."

"Wait. Ian Carpenter. I just remembered why your name sounded familiar when Brooke mentioned her cousin." Pullman's head whipped toward Ian. "You're the deputy who got shot after the Thornton investigation. The one who was undercover with them. It was all over the news." He stepped closer. "Are they back? Did you mess something up and they walked?"

"Mr. Pullman, I suggest you step down." Meadow held her arm between the manager and Ian, creating a barrier. "Ronnie Thornton died in prison three months ago, and all reports say his son was killed in an explosion. The rest of his crew were arrested or scattered in the aftermath."

Pullman never pulled his gaze from Ian's, his chest rising

and falling with ire. He looked like a man who thought Ian might be guilty of crimes he was afraid to speak out loud. Finally, he sniffed, "Maybe so, but there are girls missing in the area, just like last time. And if the Thorntons are somehow back?" He shoved his finger into Ian's face. "Then it's your hands that are covered in blood."

NINE

Meadow watched the side mirror as Rocco navigated a curve. They'd made it to the outskirts of town without picking up a tail and were heading through the mountains toward the highway. Their trip would end in even more dangerous territory, the county sheriff's office, the place Ian had been shot by one of Ronnie Thornton's hired guns.

It was also the easiest place to start searching for clues in the recent disappearances. If they could find a thread connecting them, they might be able to trace where Silas and Des had taken Brooke.

It was all they had.

In the SUV's cargo area, Cocoa and Grace rested, ready for action should they be needed.

Ian was silent. He was understandably concerned about his cousin, but it was tough to tell if he was harboring some anger that added to his silence.

If it did, Meadow couldn't blame him. The manager had blasted him for something that wasn't his fault. It had taken all of her restraint to hold her tongue.

Worse than the manager's behavior was her own. She'd essentially backed Ian into a corner and treated him like a subordinate at the crime scene. Although he'd been reckless, her actions had been disrespectful. As a colleague and a friend, she'd been wrong.

Volcanic rage had surged through her when he appeared in the doorway. What was he thinking, putting himself in harm's way? It wasn't until she'd shoved him away from the windows and felt his beating heart under her palm that the truth had struck…

She wasn't angry. She was terrified. The thought of a bullet flying through the air toward him, of losing him for real, had jerked her emotions out from under her.

The question was…why? She'd long ago buried any feelings that had surfaced while they were working together.

Yet every time he was nearby, something stirred.

Something he would never feel in return.

Rocco cleared his throat, pulling Meadow out of her spiraling. "You okay, Ian?"

Meadow turned to where Ian rode behind Rocco. His gaze met hers, steely yet pained. "I should have gotten to Brooke sooner."

"You'd be dead." Rocco was too matter-of-fact. "The point was to draw you out."

Security footage had shown the attack, and the builds of the assailants matched both Silas and Des.

"You know he's right." Meadow tried to gentle her tone. "The upside is they'll keep her alive as long as they need her as bait."

Ian frowned. "But what will they do to her?"

His concern was valid. The Thorntons hated Ian. His undercover operation had been the bomb that splintered their organization. They might take their wrath out on Brooke.

"She doesn't deserve this." Ian stared out the window. "I should surrender."

"No." The word exploded from Meadow. Even Rocco

jerked at the force of it. "They'll kill you, then her." More than anything, she wanted to touch him, to offer some comfort, but after the way her heart had twisted at the diner, she was afraid to. "Your emotions are clouding your judgment."

Hello, Pot? Meet Kettle.

"I should be doing something, not sitting here as a passenger on this road to nowhere." Ian's eyes blazed. "She's counting on me to find her, and what am I doing? I'm—"

"Doing what it takes." Rocco's voice was cool rain to Ian's raging fire. "We're going to comb through case files, pinpoint a central location, then move."

"I've got people in Missoula checking out Silas's old stomping grounds. It's possible he's headed for what's familiar." Meadow had reached out to the Marshals and local law enforcement. They had cruised by the Thorntons' former stash houses, though most had either been destroyed or auctioned. If Silas wanted to resume operations in Missoula, he would be hard-pressed to find a place.

Which meant he'd have to start over somewhere new. There were several young people missing from the surrounding areas, so what if the Thorntons were connected to all of that? "Why is Silas spending so much time around Cattle Bend?"

Rocco navigated a turn onto a two-lane road that ascended the mountain. "You thinking out loud?"

"More like brainstorming." Meadow shifted so she could look at Rocco and Ian, who still wore a mask of anger. Maybe getting him involved would help him to feel as though he was doing something constructive. "Silas can't return to any of his known locales. He's having to start fresh, which means obtaining a whole lot of property at once in order to build a network of stash houses."

"And not in his name or any known aliases." Ian sat forward, engaging with Meadow's thought process. He wore a look that said he was chasing an idea. "He'll have a shell corp or a new false identity, and he'll snap up properties somewhere that won't raise red flags."

"Somewhere like Cattle Bend." Meadow nodded. He'd boarded her train of thought.

"Okay," Rocco jumped in. "Why Cattle Bend?"

Ian leaned forward until his seat belt stopped him. "A few years ago, Cattle Bend was a dying town as coal mining dried up. The crime rate was rising. The population was moving to greener pastures. It was headed for ghost-town status."

"Until a group got together and decided to develop a new source of revenue," Meadow said. The many special elections and county meetings had made the Missoula news.

Ian nodded. "Ultimately, the town's council reached out to developers, pitching the area as an outdoorsy and artsy tourist destination like Whitefish is. Coffee shops, fishing guides, galleries... Tax breaks for small businesses brought people flocking in."

"Got it." Rocco glanced in the rearview, then joined the brainstorm. "Lots of people buying up lots of property all at once. Someone like Silas would have no problem building a network of stash houses without anyone batting an eye at the new player snatching up real estate."

"Bingo." Meadow pulled her phone from her pocket. "I'll have Isla dig into property purchases and rentals over the past two years."

"How long will that take?" It was hard to tell if the air around Ian was tight with impatience or concern.

"Hopefully not long." When Isla answered, Meadow focused her attention on the call. "It's Meadow. How fast can you can run a records search?" She ran down the events of the morning and what they were looking for.

"A couple of hours? Sooner if a pattern emerges. It'll require me to pull all of the real estate transactions for the past couple of years and to trace the purchasers to find red flags. Tough to say how long that will take. And…are you alone?"

"No. Why?" Meadow tried to decipher Isla's tone. "All good on your end?" She didn't want to attract attention, but she also wanted to know how Isla was doing. Their tech expert had been through a lot recently, and she often confided in Meadow.

She pressed the phone to her ear, trying to keep the guys from overhearing.

"All good." The words were bright.

Too bright. "Not buying it." Hopefully, the comment was vague enough for Rocco and Ian to think it was professional and for Isla to understand it wasn't. Isla clearly needed an ear.

The silence was long and void of the typical tapping that came as Isla clicked at her keyboard while she talked.

"Isla?"

"It's just…" Her teammate's sigh was heavy. "I was looking into who might have lied to the adoption agency about me having a drinking problem. I've gotten nowhere, and it's weighing on me."

"Oh." Meadow's quiet exclamation caught Rocco's attention. He pulled his gaze from the rearview to glance over with a silent question. Meadow mouthed the word *foster*.

Rocco gave a sympathetic nod, turned back to the front, then checked the rearview again. His brow furrowed, but he said nothing.

Five months earlier, Isla had been approved to foster a baby girl named Charisse. Days before the placement, an anonymous tipster told the adoption agency Isla was drinking heavily and using illegal drugs. Because of her job, the agency had been leery of the accusations but had to act, plac-

ing Charisse with another family who was now in the process
of adopting her. The events had devastated Isla and started
her on a search for who would be so cruel to her. Isla was
so good-natured and sweet that the list was short, though it
did include three ex-boyfriends and a cousin who'd cut ties
with her over a family issue.

"You came up empty on your searches?"

"All three of my exes seem to be in happy relationships,"
Isla said. "My cousin's boyfriend, the one I didn't want at
Thanksgiving after I found out he was wanted on a slew of
minor charges, is back in jail after violating parole. It wasn't
him, and she and I had a decent conversation that leads me
to believe it wasn't her either. I'm nowhere."

"I'm sorry." If only they could do more, but their resources
were focused on finding the Rocky Mountain Killer and on
the other cases they were working, including Ian's. "I wish
I could give you a hug."

Rocco shifted in his seat, drawing her attention, then
jerked his thumb toward the back window.

Dread pooled in Meadow's stomach. "Isla, I have to go."
She pocketed her phone and turned to look behind them.

Brow furrowed in confusion, Ian did the same.

A white sedan appeared around a curve, roaring toward
them at breakneck speed.

Meadow whipped toward the front. "Rocco?"

"I saw him a couple of miles ago. He was hanging back
as we came out of town, but he matched every turn I took.
Now?" Rocco gestured toward the area around them. They
were on a winding stretch of road that meandered up the
mountain before it would drop down again near the highway. No houses. No businesses. Thin traffic.

Meadow turned and let her gaze sweep past Ian to watch
the car close the distance. It disappeared briefly as Rocco

took a turn then accelerated, seeking to put distance between them.

The car appeared again, gaining on them rapidly.

They were secluded. Without backup. Meadow pulled the phone from her pocket and dialed 911. Hopefully someone would arrive quickly, because she hated the thought of a shoot-out. It was the thing she wanted to avoid the most.

But they were isolated and alone right now, and if anyone wanted to eliminate Ian, now would be the perfect time to strike a fatal blow.

Not again.

Was he really being chased through the mountains again? Silas and Des were far from creative, that was certain. Still, the threat fired adrenaline into his heart with a painful jolt. He was already wrestling with a return to the sheriff's department where he'd been shot. The last thing he needed was more stress. While he was in the capable hands of two fellow law enforcement officers and knew how to defend himself, the PTSD reared its horrible head and muddied his emotions and thoughts.

If this kept up, a heart attack would take him out before Silas ever could.

Meadow ended her call to emergency services and turned toward him. "Rocco's the best driver on our team." Her voice was tight. It was tough to tell if she spoke the truth or was simply trying to convince them all that this would end okay.

He prayed it would.

"And it's a good thing this was a drug runner's car. The engine is souped up and ready to fly." Rocco punched the gas to emphasize the statement, and they shot forward at speeds that were on the edge of sanity.

The white sedan lost ground. Ian strained to see the driver, who seemed to be alone in the vehicle. He needed to focus on the tactical, treat this like a job and not a threat to his life. No emotion. Just business.

With the way both vehicles were whipping around turns, focusing was difficult. "I can't tell if the driver is a man or a woman." He faced forward, trying to ward off motion sickness before it could kick in.

"Same." Meadow looked at Rocco. "Think they know where we're headed?"

"No." Rocco navigated another curve, his jaw tight. "If they did, they'd have waited for us there and—" Glancing in the rearview at Ian, he bit off the rest of the sentence.

Not that he had to say it. *They'd have waited for us there and ambushed us.* Just like the day he'd been shot.

He was going to be sick, and it wasn't from the wild ride through the mountains. What was he doing? Maybe he should let Meadow tuck him away in a safe house somewhere until this was over.

But no. Brooke needed him. He pulled in a deep breath and exhaled through pursed lips. There wasn't time to pull over and let him lose his breakfast. "Can you shake them?" His clenched jaw made his voice sound unnaturally deep.

"Don't need to do that. Just need to keep them at a distance until backup shows up, and we let overwhelming numbers tell them this is a very bad idea."

As if Rocco's words had spoken them into existence, two sheriff's SUVs appeared around the next turn, lights blazing and sirens blaring.

Rocco eased up on the gas. "Given that we've got their prey in our vehicle, I think the best course of action is to let the sheriff handle the chase."

"Agreed." Meadow's voice was tight.

Whipping around, Ian stared out the back window. As the

white sedan appeared around a curve, the driver slammed on the brakes at the sight of the approaching SUVs. The car spun around and, smoke spewing from the tires, roared in the opposite direction, the deputies in pursuit.

That had ended much too easily. He settled back into the seat, trying to center his emotions. "They'll try again."

"Hopefully the sheriff will catch up to them but, if not, we'll be ready for them." Meadow's gaze bored into his. "We're going to keep you safe. I promise."

It was humiliating. He should be the one offering protection, not be the one so weak that he had to receive it.

The remainder of the drive was silent. Meadow continued to face the rear, eyes focused out the back window as she watched for another tail. Rocco made it to the highway and headed west toward Summit Road, where the sheriff's department was just off the exit.

Ian stared out the side window, avoiding Meadow's eyes. He had enough roiling around inside of him without adding Meadow to the mix. Too much was happening too fast, and he desperately wished he could run back into the bunker and take shelter until this was over.

Brooke needed him, though.

As Rocco pulled off the highway exit, the imposing brick building that housed the sheriff's department came into view. He forced himself to look at it, hating the tightness in his chest. The feeling his heart was going to beat itself to death. The clamp around his lungs that kept him from taking a satisfying breath.

Now that their pursuer had disappeared, the adrenaline had subsided and left space for the memories and fears to grow. His chest felt like it might explode from the pressure the past exerted on his heart and lungs.

He forced himself to sit back and take a deep breath. There

was no way he was going to tell Rocco and Meadow he was about to come unglued. This was foolishness.

Except it wasn't.

He hadn't been to the literal scene of the crime since the day EMTs had loaded him into an ambulance and rushed him away from the parking lot where he'd been gunned down by one of Ronnie Thornton's henchmen. Ian had been hailed a hero for facing death in the race to dismantle the crime syndicate that had wreaked havoc on the area, but he'd never felt like a hero.

No, he felt more like a terrified little boy who'd been punched by a bully one too many times and had curled up in the corner to ward off the next blow.

In the past twenty-four hours, he'd been chased down a mountain and through the forest. Had been responsible for his cousin's violent kidnapping. Had been pursued once again. And he'd been shot at twice.

They'd passed his worst nightmare hours ago. A bullet flying in his direction, ripping through him before the sound of the shot reached his ears was the horror that often left his body coated in sweat.

This was the thing that might break him.

As they slowed in front of the low brick building, he tried to keep his eyes away from the scene of his near death, but his mind betrayed him and turned his gaze toward the side lot where the deputies parked their SUVs.

It was no longer visible. The chain-link fence topped with barbed wire was gone. In its place, a high brick wall shielded deputies from the street and from anyone who might want to harm them as they came and went from the building.

At least his experience had done something to protect others, but the thought was cold comfort when memories assailed him with each rotation of the SUV's tires.

As Rocco parked the car, a large iron gate came into view. Through it, Ian could see the small lot and the corner of space number seventeen, where he'd come close to taking his last breath. He had very few memories of that day, but the ones that arose shot through him like lightning, just like they did in his nightmares.

He'd just stowed his gear and shut the SUV's door when something punched him in the gut, hard. A gunshot echoed off of the building. His Sig was in his hands before he realized he'd moved, the action reflexive. Adrenaline pulsing through his veins, he'd scanned the chain-link fence as other deputies came running, shouting, their footfalls melding with the sound of his own pounding heartbeat.

There. A man stood at the fence, rifle raised, prepared to fire again. The look of cold, deadly determination in his eyes was seared into Ian's memory.

So was the need to save his fellow deputies before the shooter could pull the trigger again.

He fired.

His gunshot mingled with those from fellow deputies who'd arrived to protect one another.

Ian never saw the guy fall. Never knew whose shot ended the assault. His body had suddenly gone cold. Shivering cold. Damp warmth spread across his abdomen as his knees wobbled then dropped him to the blazing hot asphalt. He'd looked down, captivated by the dark red seeping through his shirt, across his stomach. So much red. So much… So much he couldn't connect to reality. This wasn't happening to him, was it? He was watching a movie. Reading a book. This wasn't—

"Ian?" A warm touch on his knee dragged him to the present.

Meadow eyed him with concern, her fingertips resting lightly on his kneecap.

Rocco was watching him in the rearview mirror. "You okay, man?"

Closing his eyes, Ian exhaled slowly, sliding his hand along his thigh until he found Meadow's fingers and wrapped his around hers. He'd done the same thing in the hospital, when he'd awakened to find her sitting at his bedside, her fear and concern etched in deep lines around her eyes and mouth.

Now, as then, her touch said everything was going to be okay, that he could do this.

When he opened his eyes, she was still facing him, but she was staring at their entwined fingers, her expression unreadable.

It took Ian a second to make his mouth work. His tongue was so dry. How long had he been staring into the past? Maybe he should feel embarrassment, but he couldn't muster the emotion. It was taking all he had to survive. "I'll be fine."

"You haven't been back here since that day, have you?" Meadow's fingers tightened around his.

He'd missed this. Had missed her. The way she seemed to know what he was thinking. The way her hard edges concealed and protected her soft heart, something he suspected very few people realized. He'd missed…her. The way she made him feel things no one else ever had.

He'd been thinking about her in the moment the bullet had pierced his spleen. Had been considering calling her when he got into his vehicle. A call that might have changed things between them forever. For the better if she'd accepted his invitation to an actual date. For the worse if she'd let him down easy and said their partnership had been strictly professional and she was ready to move on.

He jerked his hand from hers. How had he forgotten those

thoughts? Forgotten Meadow had been on his mind in the seconds before his life changed forever? If he'd been focused on his surroundings instead of on her, he might not have missed the gun trained on him. He might not have been responsible for putting his colleagues in the line of fire.

He'd known back then she was a risk. Relationships weren't for guys like him, who had never been taught empathy or love.

So, yeah, he didn't need to touch her or be touched by her. "I'll be fine." He repeated the words, hoping she'd buy them, then turned toward the car door. In the process, he caught Rocco's eye in the mirror, still watching, but this time his gaze held suspicion and a question.

One Ian had no intention of answering.

Instead, he scanned the immediate area, searching for danger, then forced himself to do the impossible.

He opened the car door and stepped into the bright sunlight, his feet landing on the very same pavement where he'd nearly died over eighteen months earlier, his body tense in case the Thorntons had followed him and were looking to bring his story to a not-so-poetic end.

TEN

Another conference room, another batch of files.

Five folders lay open at evenly spaced intervals around the polished wood table at the Peak County Sheriff's Department. While digital records were growing in popularity, Meadow preferred to put her hands on actual, handwritten reports.

The five folders, three thin and two thick, pierced her heart with pain and anger.

Pain. Four females and one male, ages ranging from mid-teens to early twenties, all missing.

Anger. Three had vanished after arguments with their parents. Two had been chatting with strangers online and made plans for secret meetings before disappearing.

Someone had stolen them and their innocence.

That anger layered on top of rage over that white car's pursuit of them. Had they not been in a souped-up former drug dealer's vehicle, there was no telling how that chase would have ended.

They might all be dead.

And it wasn't over. When the deputies had reported in, the news hadn't been good. The driver gained enough distance to ditch the car on the edge of town and to disappear among the crowds of tourists. Whoever had tried to hunt them down was still at large.

At the news, Rocco had walked outside with Cocoa, claiming he needed fresh air and clean headspace.

Ian sat at the end of the table, head bent over the file for eighteen-year-old Cassidy Michaels. He was buried in the work, probably using the research as a tactic to avoid emotions whipped wildly by a near-death experience in the past and too many close calls in the present.

Meadow shoved the file on seventeen-year-old Robert Moore toward the center of the table and stood, pacing to a window overlooking a courtyard. She needed to clear her mind, to stop the racing thoughts conjuring horror stories about where these kids might be and who they might be with.

To shove aside the guilt that had chased her for hours.

They'd failed the people in this area when they failed to realize Silas and Des were still alive.

How many families had been destroyed because of the Thorntons? How many more would live with terror and pain?

She dragged her hands down her face, avoiding her reflection in the glass as she stared outside.

Pressure against her knee dragged her attention to where Grace sat, leaning in as though she knew Meadow needed support.

Meadow squatted and took the K-9's face in her hands, resting her forehead against her partner's. "You just know, don't you?" She closed her eyes, letting Grace offer the comfort that only she could. It was moments like this when she realized how vital therapy dogs like their missing Cowgirl could be. Hopefully, they'd locate the labradoodle soon.

"It's rough, I know." Ian's voice came from above, low and calming.

Rocking back on her heels, she looked up at the man she'd once loved. The one who had vanished in pain and had returned to even more pain. "I'm sorry." This was her fault.

She'd been one of the leaders of the team taking down the Thorntons. If she'd done her due diligence instead of—

"Knock it off." Ian plopped onto the gray carpet beside her and rested his wrists on his bent knees. "Can I get in on the emotional support?"

Meadow smiled when Grace tilted her head toward Ian as though she'd understood his words.

Ian scratched Grace behind the ears. He'd relaxed slightly once they'd entered the conference room. Before they'd stepped inside, he'd asked for his presence to be kept quiet. Meadow had relayed the request to the sheriff, who'd shielded their way to the conference room and shut the door after a brief conversation with Ian.

She understood. What he'd experienced had been traumatic. Moving to Texas in WITSEC had left a lot of open endings. Brooke's kidnapping and the need to return to the scene of his shooting had taken an emotional toll. She couldn't blame him for not wanting to pile reunions on top of it. Even the mightiest of warriors could only take so much upheaval in one day.

She'd seen the turmoil roiling through him as they pulled into the parking lot. She'd touched his knee then immediately wished she hadn't. Her intent had been to offer comfort, but when he'd looked up at her, there had been something besides pain and fear in his expression. Something that echoed the things she'd once felt for him, things she might be feeling again, if she was being honest.

Grace shifted her attention from Meadow to Ian, angling toward him so he could more easily scratch her ears.

He seemed to be focused on the K-9, which gave Meadow the encouragement to speak freely. "I'm sorry for bringing you here. I should have considered how hard it would be."

Ian ran his hand down Grace's neck and scratched her shoulder as though he wasn't really focused on the K-9 but was seeking a distraction while he sorted thoughts. When he spoke, it was toward Grace, though the words were meant for Meadow. "I'm a big boy. If I thought I couldn't handle a ride-along, I'd have told you."

"You'd have told me, or you'd have told Grace?" The moment needed some levity.

Ian grinned. "Clearly Grace is the one in charge."

"She'd like to think so." Meadow sat back on the floor to give her knees a break and to open up a few inches of distance between them. There were things she needed to say. "I know you want to charge out there and find Brooke. So do I. But—"

"But I also know that would be the worst thing we could do. It would get me killed. Or you." Dropping his hands from Grace's neck, Ian pivoted to face Meadow. They both sat cross-legged, truly, fully face-to-face for the first time in years.

Grace lay down with her back against Meadow's hip, exhaling a contented sigh.

It was a sentiment Meadow could appreciate. Something about being in Ian's presence, alone in the quiet conference room, left her wanting to settle in and rest as well. Even with danger swirling outside the door, this space felt safe, separated from everything that was happening out in the world.

It was a foolish thought, and the kind of distraction that got people killed in the heat of battle.

But this wasn't the heat of battle. This was the four safe walls of the county sheriff's department, where they were temporarily shielded from outside threats.

Meadow didn't realize she was staring at him until his head tilted slightly, his gaze never breaking from hers. "What's going on in your head?" The question was low and gravelly, coming from somewhere deep inside of him.

It demanded the truth. Did she dare say it? "Coming here wasn't easy for me, either." She'd wanted to speak normally, but the words exhaled on a whisper. "I lost you that day."

Ian's lips flattened, his gaze turning toward the ceiling. Several emotions flashed across his face before he dipped his chin and leaned closer, his eyes capturing hers. "You really didn't."

She shouldn't be saying or feeling any of this. Meadow looked down at her fingers where they rested on her ankles. Their relationship had remained largely professional on the outside, though everyone knew they'd developed a deep friendship while they worked together. It was her heart alone that had tripped into something more, and that should be her secret to bear forever. She couldn't foist her emotions onto him. It was unprofessional. Some might say it was weak. Others would—

"Hey. Look at me." When she didn't move, Ian hesitated before he continued to speak. "I never had anybody I could count on. You know that. When I was undercover, I counted on you. I just didn't realize how much until I woke up in the hospital and…" He reached over and wrapped warm fingers around her wrist. "And you were there. The first person I saw."

Closing her eyes, Meadow dug her teeth into her top lip. She should back away, stand, get back to digging through files for answers. This was silly. They were in the middle of searching for his cousin. She was a professional, right?

Wasn't she?

So why did she come unglued whenever Ian Carpenter was around?

"You were there, Meadow, when I needed you. I'm not

used to someone caring about me. I didn't know what to do with that then." He withdrew his hand, letting the air in the room cool her wrist, but almost immediately, his fingers touched her chin, lifting her face to his.

When she opened her eyes, he was closer than he had been before, his gaze roaming her face. "I don't know what to do with that now either." He leaned in and brushed a kiss on her forehead, then rested his cheek against hers. His hand slid to the back of her neck beneath her ponytail, drawing her all the way in. He simply rested with her and breathed.

Tears stung the backs of her eyes, but she couldn't sort her emotions to figure out why. There was just Ian, this moment and something so much more intimate than the kiss she'd half thought he was about to offer. Sliding her hand along her knee, she found his free hand and held on as his fingers tightened on the back of her neck.

She let him have the moment, and she allowed herself to sink into it, wondering if he could read her mind and understand the things she wasn't saying.

Wondering if he was thinking the same thoughts. If he was, then—

A door slammed up the hallway.

They jerked back simultaneously, her head whacking the wall behind her as Ian jumped to his feet like he'd been pulled up by his collar.

Grace leaped up as well, ready for action.

Taking a deep breath, Meadow re-centered her thinking and laid a hand on Grace's head, commanding her to sit.

Rocco's voice drifted up the hallway, coming closer. "I can't believe it. I mean, if you go to the funeral home, let his family know I'm thinking of them." He appeared in the doorway pocketing his phone, his forehead creased.

"Roc?" Meadow's focus shifted to her teammate. "What's wrong?"

"Just…" He shook his head with a shudder. "There was a fire last night in Elk Valley. The former high-school baseball coach died."

"Oh, man. I'm sorry." She winced. The people of Elk Valley had already endured so much. Now this? "Did you know him well?"

"Everybody knew him. I didn't play baseball, but he taught my driver's ed class. It's just a shock on top of everything else, you know?" Reaching for the bottle of water he'd left on the table, he took a long sip. "I just need a minute."

"Sure, anything you—" A loud buzzing shattered the sentiment.

Meadow pulled her phone from her leg pocket, glancing at her screen.

Isla.

Unable to look at Ian, she focused on Rocco. "You may not get that minute. It's Isla."

Rocco nodded as Meadow answered the call. "If you have good intel, I'm sending you chocolate." Her voice was strained, but she ignored it. Hopefully, Isla would, too.

"Ooh. You know I'm always down for chocolate. But first, I know how they tracked you to your house."

"How?" They hadn't been followed. And there was no way Des or Sils had put a tracker on them.

"When we went to retrieve your SUV from the parking lot, someone had busted the window. If you had anything in there with your name on it, you'd have been a snap to track. It doesn't take much to locate someone's address online."

Meadow dropped her head back and stared at the ceiling. Really? Her vehicle? Why did the bad actors always want to mess with her vehicles? "Let's keep that quiet." Rocco would never let her hear the end of it. "So, what else have you got?"

"I've got exactly what you need." Isla's voice was grave. "Answers."

"Skyline-Horizon Properties." Rocco hooked his laptop to the big screen, and instantly, a web page appeared.

Ian admired Rocco's ability to switch gears after the news he'd received, but it was something they were all trained to do, even when it was tough to box up the feelings.

Rather than offer condolences, Ian studied the screen, attempting to clear the clutter from his mind so he could absorb what he was seeing.

They'd returned to the Cattle Bend Police Department immediately after Isla's call, needing the technology Rocco and Meadow had stored there to continue the investigation. The sheriff had promised to send copies of the files on the missing men and women to them, though they'd yielded little clear intel so far.

Skyline-Horizon might be the link they needed, though. Isla had uncovered a newcomer to the scene, one who hadn't been buying open land around Cattle Bend or other nearby towns, but who had been snatching up vacant buildings and outlying properties that held existing structures.

As Ian sat forward in his chair and braced his elbows on the table, Rocco projected a map onto the large screen. "Isla put this together, and I'm pretty sure it tells us everything we need to know."

"A picture's worth a thousand words." Meadow walked closer to the screen, and the lines around her mouth deepened as she ran her finger down a series of pins dropped on the map. "There are eleven properties. The line originates with a cluster of properties in Cattle Bend and runs almost due south with a string of individual holdings through Colorado and New Mexico to the Mexican border."

"It's a pipeline." Ian laced his fingers and held his hands together tightly. "The source is in Cattle Bend." His stomach roiled. If the Thornton syndicate was truly behind these recent land purchases, they were definitely firing up their horrifying "business" again. Given the extent of the network they were building, Brooke could be anywhere by now.

But where were they getting the money? Their assets had been frozen or seized following the initial investigation and their deaths. Either they'd hidden some accounts very well, or they had someone bankrolling them.

That question could wait. Right now, finding Brooke was the priority.

Twisting her lips to the side, Meadow studied the map. "Okay, so, let's take emotion out of the equation."

"Looks like my cue to step up. The two of you are too close to this." Rocco stepped to the other side of the screen and looked at the map, not at Meadow.

The way her head jerked toward her teammate, she'd heard the unspoken accusation as well. Rocco believed Meadow was emotionally caught up in this situation, just as Ian was. Which meant, even though he'd been distracted, Rocco had sensed the undercurrent between Meadow and Ian.

The current had almost driven him to kiss her earlier. Surely Rocco hadn't seen that. They'd been sitting on the floor out of view of the door, and Rocco hadn't returned to the room until Meadow was standing. He hadn't seen any of that moment.

But he'd likely tuned in to the emotion that had led to it. There was a thread drawing Ian to Meadow, and, the way she'd reacted, it was tugging her toward him as well. Sitting so close to her, he'd needed to make a connection, to feel something bigger than what they'd shared in the past, something that had been simmering inside of him for so long that he couldn't pinpoint when it had begun.

But it was definitely there. Her memory had chased him all the way to Texas, even when he'd done his best to forget her. It wasn't until he'd looked her straight in the eye, close enough to hear her breathe, that he realized how deeply she'd been ingrained into his thoughts. For a moment, he'd thought she might kiss him…or he might kiss her.

But he'd craved something more. Something that made a kiss feel like it would be *less than*. He'd craved simply to soak in her presence, to be close without asking anything of her. To feel…connected.

To kiss her would have been different than to simply breathe with her.

He'd never felt anything like that before. His family had left him with bruises that had never healed, scars that covered festering wounds. He'd had his share of kisses and more in a frenzied attempt to fill the void in his heart. Those encounters had never worked. They'd left him colder than ever.

But then he'd met Meadow.

No one had ever stood up for him. No one had ever cared if he lived or died. No one had ever sought to connect with him on a level that said he mattered, he had value, he was loved.

Meadow had. She saw him. Really saw him. She heard him when he spoke. Cared enough to ask how he was feeling. Put her whole life on hold to stand beside him, both in the hospital and now, when he needed her the most.

When Brooke needed both of them. No, she needed *him*. His cousin was the one other person who had, in the selflessness of her childlike love, been able to reach his heart. Now, here he was worried about his own safety and whether or not Meadow would check *yes* or *no* if he passed her a folded note.

He pulled his hands apart and shook them out, trying to loosen the tension in his fingers and to focus on the intel that might lead them to Brooke.

Meadow and Rocco stared at the screen, talking about the map in low tones.

Ian studied the blue pins dropped along a route that would drag stolen young men and women away from their loved ones and into lives of horror.

They'd stopped the Thorntons once, and it had nearly cost him his life. Could they do it again?

They had to. Those blue dots represented fear and pain and suffering. Terrors beyond comprehension.

At one of them, Brooke was likely locked away. Scared. Lost. Maybe even hurt.

Ian shot to his feet. The time for sitting still was done. They had to move. "Where is she?" The words shot out as quickly as he'd stood.

Meadow and Rocco both turned, and Meadow almost looked pained. She'd fix this if she could, he had no doubt.

He stalked to the screen and stood between them, staring at the cluster of dots in and around Cattle Bend. He jabbed his finger against the screen. "They're holding them near here. I don't think they're actively moving anyone yet."

"What makes you say that?" Rocco looked skeptical, but he was listening.

A gut instinct, mostly, but the longer Ian stared at the map and the more he considered the situation, the more he understood what his subconscious was seeing. "Hear me out…"

Meadow leaned against the wall and crossed her arms, studying him as though she could read his thoughts before he spoke them.

Ian charged ahead. "These kids all went missing within the past few months. When were these properties snapped up?"

Glancing at her phone, Meadow scrolled through the notes Isla had included with her email. "Rocco, put up the image labeled *timeline*."

The screen changed only slightly. The same map appeared, but this time, dates were posted beside each of the pins.

Ian scanned the image, certainty growing in his gut as the dots began to form a picture. There was a chance of saving Brooke and the others, but only if they moved quickly. He pointed to the cluster of holdings in Cattle Bend. "All of these were purchased six months ago, within a few weeks of each other. Because it happened during what amounts to a modern-day land grab, no one batted an eye." He dragged his finger down the map toward Mexico. "Each of these were randomly purchased during the same time period, with the last purchase only being finalized in the past week."

"I see what you're looking at." Meadow pushed away from the wall and stood beside him. Her shoulder brushed his, and he did his best to remain focused on the task at hand. "Their network may not yet be fully complete, but they're already gathering up their *inventory*." Revulsion coated the last word. Men and women like Silas and Des regarded people as objects, not as living, breathing humans. This was why they needed to be stopped, no matter the cost.

Disgust flooded Ian's veins. "There's a big gap near the New Mexico–Colorado border, which indicates they haven't completely finished their pipeline. They're missing a few key pieces."

"Which also means they're likely holding their victims in Cattle Bend, where they have more space to house them until they're able to move them." Rocco's declaration was angry, heated with loathing. "More places to move them if someone close by gets suspicious."

"Des and Silas both had time to hunt me down in the woods and to personally go after Brooke, so I doubt they're overseeing an operation with a lot of moving parts yet. They might have a henchman or two on their payroll, but it's probable they don't have a fully working organization in place." He hoped. "The trick will be figuring out which of those places they're using without Silas or Des getting wind of our presence. If they have any help at all, they'll find out quick if we roll up and do a full-on search at any location."

"It's too many places to put enough teams together to hit them all simultaneously." It was clear Meadow was thinking, but it wasn't clear the direction her thoughts were going.

"So what's the plan?" Rocco was as ready to roll as Ian was. "Obviously, we'll reach out to local law enforcement and to the feds, but I'm not certain they'll get involved yet, since we're operating on conjecture. We might be on our own a bit longer with our team tossing us a few favors."

Meadow pressed her lips into a tight line as she stared at the screen, although Ian doubted she was really seeing it. With a deep breath, she looked at Grace, who had settled onto a blanket in the corner, then turned toward Ian.

He turned as well, putting them face-to-face, trying to read her mind.

"Grace is trained to track." She said the words slowly.

Ian arched an eyebrow. Why was she telling him something he already knew?

Unless she was thinking of using Grace to sniff out each location on a quick search for the scent of one of the victims.

In a quick search for Brooke.

Which would require them to have something of Brooke's for Grace to sniff in order to track her.

Ian looked away from Meadow. If she saw the hesitation in his expression, he wasn't sure how she would handle it.

Because what she was asking of him might be close to impossible.

ELEVEN

With all of his heart, Ian wished he'd gone with Rocco in their ratty loaner SUV instead of hopping into the unmarked SUV on loan from the sheriff's department with Meadow. She'd relayed their findings to the Cattle Bend police and to the Peak County sheriff, but she'd asked them to merely pull surveillance until they could determine for certain where the Thorntons were holding their victims.

As she pulled into the driveway of his aunt's house and shifted the vehicle into Park, Ian's stomach churned. He might just be sick.

He should have sent Meadow to the house without him. The Hawletts preferred to keep their lives and their lies as far from law enforcement as possible, and they'd proven time and again that Ian and his badge represented their idea of the lowest kind of scum. Not only had he chosen a life in law enforcement, but he'd also had the audacity to be true to himself by standing up against their petty crimes.

A traitor. A turncoat. The same words Silas had used for him.

They'd called him arrogant and prideful and a moral fanatic. Every family gathering had led to him being ostracized and verbally abused, even as a child who knew they were doing wrong when they bragged about the people they'd conned.

Brooke had been cut from the same cloth as him, appalled by the family's behavior, and Ian had done his best to shield her from the cruelty they used to cover their guilt. Likely, that was the reason she'd bonded with him.

When Dean died, it had been easy for the family to heap blame on Ian for the accident he'd tried his best to prevent.

Meadow had dubbed him *Outsider* when he was undercover. She'd had no idea how right she was.

Shutting off the engine, Meadow turned to him. She'd put her badge in her pocket and had removed the identification from Grace's harness. Their plan was to approach with the least threat to his family as possible, which meant not identifying her as a marshal until it became necessary.

But Ian? They'd recognize him the minute he left the vehicle. There was no telling what kind of altercation would result.

The family was already watching. The curtains near the front door of the nondescript two-story brick house shifted and fell into place. If they hadn't already figured out who he was, they'd know soon enough. It was surprising no one had stepped onto the small front stoop with the iron railing to scream at him.

"You okay?" Meadow didn't touch him. Instead she rested her hands in her lap, studying him carefully.

Ian stared at the front of the house. "Nope." Might as well be honest. "I should be at the safe house with Rocco, not here." This was the most dangerous place he'd likely ever be, about to enter the lion's den of his family's loathing. Even bullets didn't cause as much pain as their ostracism.

"You're not who they say you are."

His head snapped toward her. What did she know of his

past? Of how he'd been cut off from everyone? How he'd been verbally beaten? What he'd endured at—

A sudden memory charged forward with almost digital clarity. He'd always remembered her beside him when he'd awakened in the hospital. Now, as though someone had opened a dam in his brain, he could hear himself under the influence of pain and medication, telling her the entire horrible story of his life. His stomach clenched. "I told you."

She merely nodded.

"All of it?"

"I don't know what *all of it* would be, but you said a lot." She looked down at her hands. "When you woke up in the hospital, you pretty much laid it all out there. I know what this is costing you today. I know Brooke means a lot to you, or you wouldn't risk walking to that front door."

Part of him was relieved someone else knew. He'd been hated and blamed, first because he looked too much like the father who'd abandoned the family, and later because he'd spoken up against the petty cons his mother and her sister were running.

And because he'd failed to stop his cousin from drinking, driving and slamming his car into a tree. That night had been the breaking point, when his aunt had screamed at him in front of an entire hospital waiting room. *Where was your goody-two-shoes behavior tonight? If you were as righteous as you pretend to be, you could have stopped this.*

His own mother hadn't even bothered to speak to him. She'd simply offered him an obscene hand gesture, then turned and walked away, not caring that he was grieving as well. That he was burdened by his own misplaced guilt.

They'd barred him from entering the funeral.

He hadn't seen them since. Only Brooke, wise beyond her young years, had reached out to him after she saw his name on a social media post. He needed his cousin in his life, and he needed to keep her safe. While he had no doubt Meadow could get what she needed from his family, the drive to rescue Brooke pushed him to be involved.

The longer he sat terrified of the past, the less time they had to secure his cousin's future.

"Let's go." Ian shoved open the door and strode toward the house, leaving Meadow to follow. He couldn't lean on her as a crutch. Some things, he had to do for himself.

She caught up quickly, having left Grace in the air-conditioned SUV. When she fell into step beside him on the sidewalk, she rested her hand between his shoulder blades. Not a word was spoken, but the silent *you're not alone* made him want to stop and pull her close, to soak in her presence until he could handle whatever came next.

They were halfway up the walk when the door flew open and a woman stepped onto the porch.

Ian stopped, shock at the sight of his aunt drawing his muscles to an immediate halt.

Tall and thin, Sylvia Hawlett was the spitting image of her older sister, Ian's mother. The only difference between them was Sylvia's dark hair, which stood in stark contrast to Rena's platinum blond. It was clear Sylvia dyed it to hide her age, as it seemed unnaturally dark. She was still trim and well put together, a trait her sister had never shared.

Her perfectly made-up face was contorted in rage when she stalked down the steps toward Ian. "You have more of a spine than I thought, showing up here today." She spat the words with enough venom to burn a man on contact.

Ian stopped walking as each syllable blistered his skin. He said nothing. As often as he'd endured the wrath of the Hawletts, it shouldn't still sting.

But it did.

Beside him, Meadow stood still, her posture relaxed. It was a tactic to keep the enemy off guard. Beneath her poise, she was coiled and ready to strike if the situation warranted action.

A small group of people stood inside the doorway, watching the scene unfold, but none of them triggered immediate recognition. They could have been strangers, though he had no doubt it was his own flesh and blood waiting for him to be gutted in the arena of battle.

Sylvia stopped six feet away, her fists clenched at her sides. "Where is my daughter?" The hissed question dripped with the poison of her hatred.

Meadow responded before Ian could. "That's what we're here to find out, Ms. Hawlett."

The wrath turned to Meadow. "And who are you? If you're defending him because you're dating him, then you should know the kind of man he—"

"Enough." Attacking Meadow was more than Ian would allow. "*Deputy Marshal* Ames is investigating Brooke's disappearance." It didn't matter any longer if they knew Meadow was in law enforcement. His family had run roughshod over him, but he would not allow them to disrespect her, not while he could do something about it.

His aunt's gaze swung back to him, and her voice dropped impossibly lower. "You brought a US Marshal into this?"

He bit down on the words *she's a friend*. That would only serve to drag them back to his aunt's initial suspicions.

"I don't know why you bothered." Sylvia's chin tipped up, and her haughty expression reset itself. Even in the face of her daughter's disappearance, she wallowed in disdain for her only nephew. "I have every idea you know where my daughter is. I was about to call the sheriff about you, but you've saved me the trouble." She turned to Meadow. "Deputy, there's no need to investigate further. This man took my daughter. He's the one you need to arrest."

The hardest fight of Meadow's life was the one she currently waged within herself. It was taking all she had to hold her expression at neutral. She swallowed the words she wanted to fire at Ian's *aunt* and opted to stare the woman down instead.

The first to look away would lose.

Sylvia blinked, turning to Ian. "I know you have Brooke. Coming here is a way to cover your—"

"Ms. Hawlett." Meadow hit the name hard. "That's enough. There isn't a shred of evidence to point to Ian being involved with Brooke's disappearance." After her earlier comments about them dating, there was no way she was going to tell this woman Ian had been with her at the time of the abduction.

"He's been in contact with my daughter against my wishes. We've found emails on her laptop and are looking at our cell phone bill now to see if the number she's been texting belongs to him. Reaching out to young women in secret. Isn't that how all *predators* behave?"

Ian flinched. The blow had landed.

Meadow spoke before he could say something that would express either his hurt or his anger and turn this situation even more volatile. "Mr. Carpenter has a solid alibi, and we know about the communication between him and your daughter, which is completely aboveboard." They'd combed through the emails and texts the night before, searching for clues. "We're here because I'm a K-9 officer, and we'd like to see if we can locate your daughter by tracking her. The county doesn't have that capability, and I'm offering my services. We believe, given something of your daughter's that would allow my partner to follow a scent, we can locate Brooke."

Sylvia Hawlett stared at Meadow, her expression as sharp and rigid as a knife. It was possible she was about to kick them off of the property.

Meadow didn't break eye contact.

Without warning, Sylvia's chilled demeanor melted. Her jaw slacked, and tears stood in her eyes. She began to shake. "My daughter... You could find my daughter?"

Compassion softened Meadow's anger. No matter what the Hawlett family had done, this was a woman whose daughter had been violently kidnapped. She was worried and afraid, and that deserved a measure of mercy and concern. Meadow glanced at Ian.

His head had tilted to the right slightly, and he eyed his aunt's breakdown with a practiced expression, almost as though he was judging the authenticity of the emotions. The opposite of his aunt's demeanor, his jaw was tight and his shoulders rigid, as though he was holding himself back.

When he caught Meadow's eye, she gave him a brief nod. This moment was his to navigate. She prayed God would use it to begin to heal him and his family, knowing that was the kind of work only God could do. If nothing else, she prayed this moment would be one of compassion.

With a soft exhale, Ian tentatively laid a hand on his aunt's shoulder.

She immediately stepped toward him, accepting his embrace as she cried on his chest. "I just... I just want her to... to be safe."

Ian's eyes slipped shut, and while his posture remained stiff, he accepted his estranged aunt's grief.

Unwilling to intrude upon a moment when God was clearly at work, Meadow scanned the area. No one came out of the house, although they could be seen at the storm door and the front windows. It seemed the Hawletts weren't willing to extend a proverbial olive branch to Ian, even given the pressing nature of the situation.

The house was well-kept and spoke of money. Not millionaire kind of money, but a comfortable living. From Ian's stories, she knew their income had come largely from conning tourists in nearby Whitefish, bilking charitable people online and embezzling from various organizations. There had never been enough proof for the Hawletts to be brought to justice. Even Ian's testimony couldn't be counted on to bring them punishment for their crimes.

Now wasn't the time. Time was of the essence if they wanted to find Brooke before the Thorntons pushed her down their pipeline and into oblivion.

Meadow cleared her throat as Sylvia's storm of tears subsided.

The older woman sniffed and backed away from Ian, smoothing her floral shirt as though she was dusting away contaminants. She didn't look at her nephew. Instead, she faced Meadow and swiped the tears from her cheeks. "What do you need, Deputy Marshal?"

So that's how it's going to be. The woman had stormed her tears onto her nephew yet offered him no grace in return? In a different situation, Meadow would have so many words for—

Baby steps. The words sank into her mind, coming from who knew where, although she suspected God was admonishing her. Let Him work it out. It wasn't her job to pull an apology from the Hawletts or to broker a reconciliation Ian might not want. Her sole task was to bring Brooke home safely.

She swallowed her emotions and cleared her throat. Normally she had a whole spiel she went through, but today she didn't have the energy. "I need something Brooke has worn recently and often. Or, if you haven't changed the sheets on her bed, her pillowcase would work well. The more contact she's had with the object, the more it will hold a scent." She pulled out an evidence bag she'd stowed in her back pocket. "If you can take me to the object, I can—"

"No." The edge returned to Sylvia's expression, though it was not as sharp as before. "I don't give law enforcement permission to enter my home." She held out her hand, palm up. "If you give me the bag, I'll bring something out to you."

That was perfectly within her rights. Since the bag was meant merely to preserve the scent and not to protect evidence, the request wasn't problematic, though it was annoying.

Meadow passed the bag to her with quick instructions on the best way to collect the item without muddying the scent, then walked toward the SUV when Sylvia disappeared through the front door.

Ian leaned against the passenger door with his arms crossed, staring at the house next door.

Giving him a minute, Meadow continued to watch the front of the Hawlett house. What was going on in there that required such vigilance from those inside? What were they afraid she'd see if she walked in?

"Whatever they're hiding, it's of the white-collar crime variety." Ian's voice was low, grating across the words. "Likely the only reason she wouldn't let you in is fear something incidental might incriminate them, not because they're actively in the process of committing a crime." His forehead creased. "And, you know, they don't want to risk getting the stench of me into their inner sanctum."

"Ian…" She moved to touch him, but with prying eyes on them, that wasn't the best idea if she wanted to maintain the sense of professionalism they'd cultivated. Still, his pain crossed the distance between them to rest like a heavy mantle on her shoulders. "I know this isn't easy."

"I shouldn't have come. It made everything harder. You'd have had an easier time if I hadn't been a distraction."

"I doubt it. I think you jolted your aunt out of the emotional box she's built. Seeing you threw her off-balance. She never would have broken down in front of me and might have denied me completely. At least—"

"Don't say it." He pushed away from the truck and paced a few steps to the edge of the driveway, still staring at the next-door neighbor's house. "She only accepted comfort from me because I was convenient. Believe me, if she'd been anywhere near her right mind, she'd have put a fist in my face instead. It wouldn't be the first time."

The front door opened, and Sylvia appeared.

Ian walked to the rear of the vehicle and out of sight before Meadow could react to his stark declaration. The last thing he needed was another interaction with his aunt, even one of indifference.

Meadow met Sylvia on the sidewalk and took the bag, which now held a light blue sweater. "I can't promise this will be returned to you."

"Just find my daughter." Sylvia had reverted to the clipped anger she'd displayed initially, but her gaze drifted to the vehicle, lingering where Ian stood out of sight. Something seemed to soften, and she looked back to Meadow. "Thank you." Without waiting for a response, she turned and walked into the house, shutting the door firmly behind her.

TWELVE

The sound of his aunt's sobs lingered in Ian's ears as they pulled into Cattle Bend on the main road. Her willingness to let him comfort her had shocked him. Her quick reversal into icy disdain had been expected.

Still, the chill had burned in a special way, coming after a moment when someone in his family had touched him for the first time in years. What was he supposed to do with that? Go back to the status quo? How? Brooke was missing. It would be so much easier if the family could pull together during the search, but it was clear that wasn't going to happen.

The SUV had been silent for the twenty-minute ride to town. Ian was mortified at the things he'd confessed to Meadow, including the physical abuse he'd endured at the hands of his mother and aunt. That was the one thing he kept buried, the one thing he never dwelled on even in his lowest, darkest times. The memories had clearly been there, festering, because they had bubbled up in a horrible moment of confession.

Meadow slowed as they neared the diner, where crime-scene tape fluttered in the breeze that funneled up the narrow street. Several official vehicles remained on the sidewalk as the crime-scene team gathered evidence.

"Which site are we going to go to first?" He needed to say something. If he didn't, he'd demand Meadow pull over so he could charge into the diner. A weird glitch in his brain wondered if he could turn back time and rescue Brooke before the abduction occurred. There was another irrational part of him that believed he could walk into the restaurant and find Brooke waiting for him as they'd planned.

"The bank building at the corner of Reyes and Third. Since it has a vault..."

A vault. What was happening to Brooke as they drove around searching for her? What horrors was she enduring?

He should have seen her immediately and not let Silas and Des chase him into the hills. If he had, he could have stopped whatever nightmare she was currently fighting to survive.

Meadow didn't seem to notice he was battling waves of nausea over his responsibility for Brooke's plight. She didn't even look at the diner as she cruised to the end of the street and took a left into an older section of town where revitalization had been slower. Several small restaurants and shops were already bringing life to pockets between vacant storefronts, so it wouldn't be long before this area was hopping as well. For now, it was a hodgepodge of old and new, of vibrant life and eerie desolation.

At Reyes and Third, Meadow rolled to a stop at the sign and surveyed the front of the old Cattle Bend Savings and Loan. The three-story brick building stood silent sentry, its windows covered with brown paper on the inside and the doors chained shut on the outside. "Local law enforcement has cruised by this site looking for signs of activity, but they haven't attempted to engage. The last thing we want is to send in the cavalry to the wrong place and put the Thorntons on alert."

There was no telling what they'd do to Brooke and the others if they realized their safe houses had been compromised. They'd either move immediately or...

Or do something so much worse.

Turning left, Meadow drove past the alley behind the bank. Trash littered the area, and construction debris from the storefront next door crowded the space. A couple of men in paint-spattered clothes stood near a doorway farther down the alley, clearly taking an early afternoon break.

Was this the place? His intuition said no. "It's not likely they'd use a stash house near a busy worksite. There's too much risk of being seen or heard by the crew doing renovations."

"You're probably right, but I'm still wondering about that vault."

A bank vault would likely be dark, airless and soundproof. He didn't want to think about Brooke locked away behind a heavy steel door, panicked and fighting for breath. "There's a camera mounted above the door of the shop next to the bank. I seriously doubt Silas would bring his victims into a space with built-in surveillance."

"Unless it's his surveillance." Meadow was deep in thought as she parallel parked in front of a coffee shop up the street from the bank. She tapped the steering wheel as she stared out the windshield. "I want to get Grace out with her super sniffer and walk back to the bank, see if she picks up on anything. I'll talk to those workers and see if they've noticed suspicious activity or heard anything that concerns them."

There was no way he was sitting on the sidelines. Ian reached for the door. "I'm going with—"

"No, you're not." Laying a hand on his bicep, Meadow tugged gently, pulling him back into his seat. "You're highly recognizable to Silas and Des and to anyone they've managed to hire onto their crew. One look at you snooping around a building they own and they're going to know we're onto them." She pointed out the windshield. "The diner is at the end of the street in your direct line of sight. If you're spotted, they'll think you're here because the diner is here, not because we're checking out the bank." Her grip tightened. "I know this is hard. I know you want to take action. You love your cousin and want her to be safe. This is the only way."

Anger surged through Ian. He hated being chained up. Hated being the catalyst for Brooke's suffering. Hated that Meadow was right. As much as he wanted to be in the open kicking down doors, he was a hindrance, not an asset. "Take me to the safe house, then you can investigate without me getting in the way."

Was he whining? Because even to his own ears, it sounded like he was whining.

Meadow arched an eyebrow. "I know you. If you were locked up in a safe house, you'd go stir-crazy and wind up taking matters into your own hands. You'd last about thirty minutes, tops. Besides…" She released his arm and reached for her door, effectively turning her back to him. "I need you with me."

She was out of the SUV with the door closed behind her before Ian could process what she'd said.

She needed him.

He stared out the window but saw nothing, drowning in her brief confession as she opened the rear lift gate, leashed Grace and allowed her to sniff the sweater, then headed down the street.

Meadow needed him.

Other than on the job, he was pretty sure no one had ever needed him before. And, really, had the job needed him? He'd disappeared into WITSEC, and the sheriff's department hadn't fallen apart. His family had certainly never needed him as anything other than their whipping boy. Brooke hadn't needed him, even though she'd reached out and kept in touch with him and had loved him as her family.

But *need*?

Meadow was a woman who had it all together. Who charged into life and took care of business while having compassion for victims and their families. She possessed a strong faith, a strong family and a strong friend group. She was not someone who needed to lean on another person.

But him? He'd drawn strength from her in the hospital and in this current trial. He had unknowingly been bolstered by her memory when he'd started over in Texas. He'd called her when he was in danger, and she'd come running.

He needed her, but he'd never considered the sentiment might run both ways.

What could Meadow possibly need him for? He couldn't offer her anything. He had no real home. No sense of family and, honestly, no sense of identity outside of his work. When it came to having something of value, he was definitely the least of everyone on the planet. No worth. No purpose.

Worth. Purpose. When he'd started going to chapel with the rodeo, those words had been tossed around quite a bit by the guys who led the services. Ian had scoffed at them. God existed, but what did He need a guy like Ian for? Why would He care what happened to a guy whose family didn't even love him? God had created him, sure, but then He'd taken His hands off and let Ian run the race alone.

Except…

Brooke loved him. Meadow seemed to care. If they could find some nugget of value in him, then maybe there was something to that verse Hayden, one of the younger guys, had stitched onto his chaps. Something about God knowing all of his days before he was born and writing them down in a book.

If that was true, then God was well aware of everything that would happen to Ian in his life. The shooting. The family trauma. Everything.

Maybe God wasn't so hands-off after—

A shadow fell across the interior of the car.

Something hard tapped on the passenger window.

Ian whipped toward the sound and stared straight down the barrel of a pistol.

Lord, if we could find Brooke at this first location... It was a desperate prayer, but one Meadow sincerely hoped God would answer. The minute hand was spinning faster, and the longer they took to find the stash house, the more hope of finding Brooke and any other victims diminished.

Grace didn't alert along the sidewalk, though she kept her nose to the ground and sniffed away, diligent in her job and wanting the treat that came from successfully completing an assignment.

Meadow watched her and also scanned the surrounding buildings as she plotted a strategy for approaching the men in the alley. When it came to disarming potential suspects or witnesses, sometimes the best thing to do was to play to the stereotype. *Girl who needed help with her runaway dog* gave her a defenseless air, one that tended to win over both men and women if it was played right.

At the corner near the alley, Meadow slowed and allowed Grace to see the men. She crouched beside her partner and unhooked the leash from the K-9's unmarked harness. "Grace. Greet."

With a joyful leap, Grace bounded up the alley toward the workers, tongue lolling like a happy pup on a romp.

Meadow waited a beat before pursuing, purposely calling her by the wrong name and using the wrong commands.

"Tally! Stop! Leave those men alone!" She waved her arms. "She's safe, I promise. Just friendly. Can you grab her?"

The men stepped into the center of the alley to block Grace's path, and the dog leaped onto the younger one's chest, then dropped down to roll onto her back as though all she wanted was belly rubs from her new friends.

The older of the two workers chuckled. Shoving his hat back on his head, he squatted and obliged Grace with a belly rub with one hand as he grabbed the handle on her harness with the other. "Looks like she got away from you."

Meadow approached, pretending to be breathless from the chase. She passed the leash to the man holding Grace's harness, then leaned forward with her hands on her knees as though she needed to catch her breath. "She jumped out of the SUV before I could leash her. She's a little escape artist."

The man clipped her leash, then handed the end to Meadow as he stood. "I wouldn't call her *little*. What is she? Looks like a Weimaraner but her color's wrong."

"Yeah, I guess she's not so small anymore." Meadow smiled as she looped the leash around her arm. "She's always going to be my baby. And she's a vizsla. You know your dogs if you thought she looked like a Weimaraner. They're cousin breeds and often confused."

"My brother has a Weimaraner. Pretty dogs."

The alley was darker than the sun-soaked street, though the temperature was hotter here where no breeze stirred. It smelled of paint, sawdust and stale air. Meadow looked around as though she was seeing the alley for the first time. "Sorry to bother you guys. I was going to walk her up the main street, but it looks like the police are doing some kind of investigation. You guys working on one of the stores or something?" The easiest way to get information was to play ignorant.

"Yeah. Lots of sirens earlier. Not sure what it was about, though." The younger guy stepped up. He was younger than she'd initially thought, probably only sixteen or seventeen, and he had all of the youthful swagger that would make him think he could impress the ladies. "I thought about walking over there and seeing what was up, but my grandpa needed my help, so I hung around here."

Meadow almost smiled but bit back the grin and snapped her fingers to call Grace to heel. There was no need to encourage the kid.

Not that he needed it. He kept right on talking. "We're about to open an organic butcher shop. We have a small farm outside of town. Beef and pork and some truck."

"Truck?"

"Vegetables." The older man practically rolled his eyes at his grandson and gave Meadow a slight, apologetic smile. He knew what was up. "We've always sold at the farm, but with the town growing and us being a good half an hour away, we figured we'd give it a shot."

"That sounds cool. I'll have to check it out." There were several small farms around the area that sold to the public, but since she didn't actually cook, she'd never paid them much attention.

Rocco would love a place like this. It had all of the farm-to-table things he enjoyed so much. She could really afford to learn a few cooking tricks from him, but that wasn't why she was here. There was so much more than her cholesterol at stake.

She scanned the alley and let her gaze linger on the bank. "Anything going on in this building? Looks like it's ready for something to go into it as well."

The younger man shrugged. "Dunno. We heard some corporation bought it, but nobody's been around since we've been here working. It's been quiet. We're all waiting to find out. Lots of people convert old banks into restaurants or wedding spaces, so who knows?"

"I hope it's a restaurant." The grandpa arched an eyebrow. "If it is, maybe we can cut a deal with them as exclusive suppliers or something. Restaurants and grocery stores are where the real money is."

It was clear she wasn't going to get much information out of the two of them. She'd gotten what she needed anyway. The bank could be crossed off their list. "Well, I wish you the best." Meadow clucked to Grace, who stood, ready for action. "I'm going to get this energetic little girl moving so maybe she'll calm down this afternoon. It was nice meeting you."

"Same to you." The older man shoved his grandson toward the rear of their store before the young man could speak. It was clear grandpa understood the awkward flirting and was putting a stop to it in a quiet way.

Yeah, Grandpa was going to have his hands full with that kid.

Meadow bit back a grin.

As soon as they disappeared into the building, Meadow knelt in front of Grace and pulled the bag containing the sweater from her backpack. She let her partner have a good sniff, then gave her the command to search.

Grace inspected the area as they walked toward the street, nosing around in trash piles and construction debris, but she never alerted, not even at the door to the bank. Clearly, this wasn't the site they were looking for.

At the alley's entrance, she knelt, passed Grace a treat and praised her work, then turned toward the borrowed SUV. It would be good to have her K-9 SUV back with all of the comforts and alarms for Grace. Traveling incognito had its downsides, but they'd have to deal with those as they headed to the next location, an old hardware store on the outskirts of town.

As she stood, the shadow of a person moved on the sidewalk at the passenger side of the vehicle. Had Ian once again disobeyed what amounted to an order and stepped into the open? It would be so like him to—

Someone moved in the passenger seat. No, Ian was still right where she'd left him.

Meadow commanded Grace to heel then reached for her sidearm at her hip. It could be innocent, someone asking for directions or curious about the commotion at the diner.

Or they could have stepped straight into the lion's den… and she'd left Ian without backup.

She fought to keep her pace steady, not wanting to draw attention to herself. If Silas and his crew were watching, they'd know she was nearby. She might be less recognizable to them than Ian was, but they'd still figure out she was with him if she made a wrong move. She kept Grace on the opposite sidewalk as though they were simply strolling around town. She prayed for Ian's safety and that they could get out of this alive.

Sliding the leash to her wrist, she pulled out her phone and thumbed a quick text to Rocco, asking him to contact the Cattle Bend PD. They were close, just a few hundred feet away at the diner, so backup could reach them quickly. As soon as Rocco confirmed, Meadow pocketed her phone and walked past the SUV, not looking toward it although she watched it from the corner of her eye.

There was definitely someone standing near the passenger door.

At the corner, she crossed the street, allowing her to get a good look at Ian's position.

Her stomach sank as adrenaline surged.

A man she didn't recognize stood close to the door. It was clear he was armed, though the way he stood shielded the weapon from view.

He could pull the trigger any second.

It was time to drop all pretense.

Commanding Grace to stay, Meadow dropped the leash and ran toward Ian. "Ian! Duck!" She raised her weapon. "Federal agent! Drop your weapon!"

The man startled and whirled toward her, his pistol aimed straight at her center mass.

A gunshot cracked before she could fire.

THIRTEEN

Ian shoved the door open as hard as he could, knocking his attacker sideways as the man pulled the trigger. The shot he'd fired at Meadow exploded against the building beside them, raining brick debris to the sidewalk.

The man stumbled and almost went down. It wasn't much, but it was enough.

Ian was out of the vehicle and around the door before the man could regain his footing. He drove an uppercut into the assailant's jaw, whipping his head backward.

The gun clattered to the ground. The man's dark eyes glazed as he wavered, dropped to his knees, then pitched forward onto his face.

Kicking the gun toward Meadow, Ian looked down at the man he'd bested. The man who'd pointed a gun at his face. The man who could have killed him…and Meadow.

He'd been only inches from the gun this time. Inches from the bullet that could have ended everything.

Nausea tried to double him over. As quickly as his energy had surged, it flagged, dragging the strength from his joints in a tidal wave of fear.

A pistol. He'd faced down the barrel of a pistol. Again.

Ian gulped air. Training had kicked in and allowed him to take down the bad guy, but in the aftermath, he stared into his worst nightmare. His pulse rate shot up. His breaths quickened. His superheated skin sheened with sweat.

As Meadow pressed a knee into the man's back and dragged his arms behind him to cuff his wrists, she looked up at Ian. "Sit. Now. Breathe. Head between your knees. Breathe, Ian!"

The words cut through the darkness swirling at the edges of his vision and beat their way through the roar in his ears. He dropped to the seat of the SUV and leaned forward.

From his left, shouts and pounding footsteps approached, but he couldn't see around the door. Sound and sight blended into one sense, a cacophony of noise and light that his brain refused to process. He simply stared at the curb beneath his feet and focused on breathing. *In. Out.*

Voices and motion swirled, then the SUV rocked as the lift gate opened and shut.

Then…Meadow. She sat on the curb in front of him, looking up into his face. "How's it going?" Her voice was soft and comforting. She reached up and laid her hands against his cheeks. They were cool against his warm skin, easing some of his fear and drawing him back into reality.

Horrifying, humiliating reality.

He'd panicked in front of her.

As the fog cleared and his senses settled, inadequacy screamed in his head. The very worst of his weaknesses, the largest failure inside of him, had torn loose and roared out to be witnessed by the person he wanted to impress the most.

Her thumb stroked his cheek, and her gaze held his. "Thanks for saving my life. I might have hesitated to fire in the middle of town like this."

She was lying. Meadow was a crack shot who wouldn't have missed her target.

Behind her, several Cattle Bend police officers hauled the man to his feet, though he wobbled from the blow Ian had dealt. One officer stepped closer. "We're going to have him checked out by the paramedics then take him to the station. You need medical transport?"

"No." Meadow dropped her hands to Ian's knees as she looked up over her shoulder at the officer. "We'll be there shortly. I want to see him questioned as soon as he's processed. He might know where Brooke Hawlett is being held." She started to turn back to Ian, then stopped. "Hey, do you have enough manpower to post someone about twenty feet away from us until we roll out?"

"Sure do." The officer motioned to one of the men, then they all disappeared from Ian's line of sight.

Ian let his head fall forward. "I let the guy sneak up on me."

"I left you alone." Meadow tightened her grip on his knees. "This isn't your fault. We're doing the best we can, but our best isn't good enough when we don't know what we're up against. Your timing was perfect just now. You saved me and maybe even someone out on the main street if that bullet had made it past me." She angled her head until he had no choice but to focus on the sincerity in her expression. "Ian, you're still trained in law enforcement. You're still *you*. Your instincts kicked in, and you came through for everyone. Fear is natural. It's nothing to be ashamed of. Nobody faults you for not wanting to take a beating from a lead fist again."

Thoughts spun in his head, and emotions raced through his heart. Ian closed his eyes, trying to shut out the external stimuli, focusing on Meadow's touch instead. She was the one person he wanted to impress…

But she was clearly the one person he didn't *have* to impress.

She already believed in him. Already saw a hero in him, just as he saw one in her.

She didn't fault him for his weakness. She didn't even view his fear as weakness. She embraced him for who he was, scars and all.

He hadn't cowered when he'd come face-to-face with a pistol's barrel. He hadn't flinched when Meadow was in danger. He'd reacted. He'd protected. Only in the aftermath had he come unglued.

Maybe he was healing after all.

Inhaling deeply, he opened his eyes and found Meadow still looking up at him.

Life. Survival. They surged through him. He was truly healing, had truly survived another close encounter with death.

Maybe the cowboys at the rodeo were right. Maybe God had something for him and was keeping him on this earth, putting one foot in front of the other, for a reason.

Maybe...

He was caught up in Meadow's blue eyes, so close. So sincere. So...alive.

He had the irrational urge to kiss her. To drive home the truth he was alive and so was she, and maybe there was something on the other side of this for him. For *them*.

Meadow's head tilted slightly, and her expression softened.

But then, so fast he wondered if he'd imagined the moment, her mood shifted to a no-nonsense, all-business investigator facade. Patting his knees, she stood. "If you're good, we need to get to the courthouse, where the police department is. We made a spectacle of ourselves out here, and now we've apparently got one of Silas's men in custody. Word's going to get back to him fast. While he'll likely think we were here because of the crime scene at the diner, we don't need him getting suspicious about our presence before we can recon the rest of the sites." Tapping the door with her fist, she walked away and spoke to the officer standing guard.

Ian watched as he turned in his seat and shut the car door, forcing himself away from his heart and into his mind. They had a job to do. He had a cousin to rescue.

Meadow had been right earlier. The man who'd tried to kill them might know where Brooke was. That needed to be his primary focus.

That and the truth… He was still a man without a family. One who didn't know how to love.

One who would never be worthy of a woman like Meadow Ames.

On the other side of the one-way glass, Van Moore stared at the detective across the table from him with steely eyes. Other than asking for a lawyer, the thug who'd taken a shot at Meadow hadn't said a word since they'd led him into interrogation.

It was taking all of Meadow's restraint not to charge into the room television-detective style and back Van's smug self against the wall with her forearm against his throat.

Ian stood stiffly beside her, likely battling similar thoughts. "He knows something." He ground the words through clenched teeth. "And I'm willing to guess he's the one who was chasing us through the mountains after we left the diner."

"Both of those things are likely, but we have no leverage to get him to talk. As far as we know, there's nothing that makes him more afraid of us than he is of Silas or Des." The two were known to be ruthless. The Thorntons had proven they could reach anyone, even behind prison bars. Before his death, Ronnie had ordered hits on several of his former henchmen who had been arrested after the initial raid. Officials were still trying to figure out who had fed him information and how he'd been able to have them killed in jail.

Now that they knew Silas and Des were alive, the *who* was obvious. The *how* might forever remain a mystery.

"How long before you hear back from your people?" Ian stared intently through the glass as though he could will Van to speak. "Maybe we need to let him sit here and stew while we go out and keep searching."

But where would they search? There were no signs of life at any of the other locations law enforcement had surveilled. "Look, Isla's good at what she does. She'll get back to us fast." Meadow had passed on everything the police had given her about Van. Isla could dig up intel faster and search deeper than a local PD. "Also, I'm not so sure about taking you out with me again. It might be time for both of us to move to the safe house and to let others do the footwork."

"No." Ian looked at her for the first time since they'd entered the small room. "I want to be involved, not tucked away somewhere consuming oxygen while other people take on the risk for me."

Meadow dug her teeth into her tongue and counted to ten while she formulated her next words. "You could have died today."

"So could you."

She likely would have if he hadn't reacted so quickly, but that wasn't a thought she could allow to settle if she wanted to stay focused. "Rocco can take point on the search while you and I take a breather at the safe house. Three other members of my team are on the way here to help out. They'll be here late tonight."

"Those are wasted hours Brooke probably doesn't have."

He didn't need to keep telling her. The time bomb ticked in her brain so loudly it was shocking the clicks didn't echo off the walls in the small room.

On the other side of the glass, neither the detective nor

Van had moved in what felt like hours. They both sat back in their chairs with their arms crossed over their chests, staring at one another as though waiting for the other to blink first.

"Aren't you going to do something?" Ian turned fully toward her, his hands clenched at his sides. "I can't stand here. There's got to be—"

Meadow's phone buzzed, the soft sound loud in the cramped room. With a hard look to stem any more of Ian's words, she pulled it from her pocket and held it up to show him Isla's video call request. "She's got something."

"Finally."

Tightening her jaw to keep from defending her friend by reminding him it had been less than an hour, Meadow tapped the screen so Isla's face appeared. "You're on the line with me and Ian."

"Anybody else?" Isla leaned closer to the phone she kept in an elevated stand on her desk by her computer screen, her brunette ponytail swinging. She likely had intel she didn't want overheard.

"Nope. We're in interrogation watching the silence on the other side of the glass."

Isla sat back in her chair, allowing a broader view of her office behind her. "I'm not surprised he's being stoic and silent. Van Moore is hard-core. I'm surprised Silas was able to get him on the payroll, to be honest. His services don't come cheap."

"Great." Venom laced Ian's soft exclamation.

Venom that Meadow could almost taste in her own words. "So Silas and Des might be further along in building up their network than we initially thought?"

"Tough to say?" Isla rarely expressed such uncertainty. "They could have thrown all of their eggs into the Van Moore basket, making him their only muscle. It's interesting, though…" She leaned closer with a glint in her eye that said she had tantalizing tea to spill. "Van Moore and Desiree Phelps do *not* get along. It seems they were a bit of a couple at one time…until she double-crossed him after a job they pulled together before she worked for Ronnie Thornton. She wanted all of the take for herself. She hung him out to dry, and Van spent a couple of years in prison before he was released on a technicality."

"That's definitely cause for bad blood." Ian winced, his anger fading as they made progress with new information.

"Yet it appears Silas has him on the payroll?" That made no sense. Des was Silas's right hand. She'd been with the Thornton organization from the beginning. Why would Silas hire someone who would cause friction within the group when they were navigating a rebuild? "We're sure Van is working for the Thorntons?" Was it possible there was another player in the game?

"I was able to access Van's phone records, and I already had Silas's from our earlier search. Des's, too. Silas has been in contact with Van repeatedly over the past month or so. Des? Not once."

"None of this adds up." What was Silas doing? The only way this made sense was if Des had somehow crossed Silas, and he was looking to cut her out by hiring different muscle, or… "Hey. When did Van Moore get out of prison? Before or after Des faked her death?"

"Hang on." Isla's focus shifted to the left, toward her computer screen. She typed then scrolled. "Looks like he got out about three months after." Her gaze shifted back to the phone, a sly smile lifting one corner of her mouth. "He probably believed Des was dead, so he never exacted his revenge."

"Now he knows she's alive, so he's ready to move. I'm thinking Silas is up to something." It was possible Silas was playing his most trusted associate and her most hated enemy against one another to gain an unknown advantage. But what? "Who are Van Moore's other known associates? Let's look at his more recent activities, just before he hitched his wagon to Silas."

Going back to her computer, Isla's eyes shifted as she read. "Most of the intel I dug up has him around Chicago until he fell off the grid around the same time he started talking to Silas. I've got surveillance images of him with the Biancos, some of it going back several years." Grabbing her phone, she held it so they could see the stills from security-camera footage on her screen.

Ian leaned in to get a better look, his shoulder brushing Meadow's. "What are the Biancos known for?" Dread seemed to drag his words down, as though he already knew.

Meadow had a sick feeling her thoughts matched his. "It's human trafficking, isn't it?"

Her expression grim, Isla nodded. "They started out in drugs decades ago, setting up pipelines through the Canadian border. Drugs are a one-time commodity, though. You sell your inventory, it's gone, and you have to obtain more."

"People are different." Ian spat the words and walked to the glass, though Meadow doubted he saw anything on the other side. "You can sell them for a one-time payment, or you can rent them out over and over again for a steady stream of income."

It never failed to sicken her, the absolute disregard for human life and spirit. How criminals treated living, breathing humans as products. It was heartless and cold and downright evil. *Oh, Jesus...* There was no other prayer.

Her stomach turned in on itself. Even if they rescued Brooke, there were thousands upon thousands of others around the world suffering the horrors of modern-day slavery. There was no way to rescue them all.

She needed to focus on the ones she could help before she drowned in futility. Meadow glanced at Ian, whose posture was rigid not in anger, but in pain. They had to rescue Brooke or he'd never survive the guilt he had imposed upon himself.

She forced her mind onto the job, onto the trail of what Silas might be up to. "It's likely Silas has partnered with Van, who has access to resources with the Biancos that can help him spin up his operation faster."

"Right."

Ian stepped back into the conversation. "So either Silas is double-crossing Des and has promised to hand her over to Van once he gets what he wants…"

"Or Silas and Des are making Van believe he's being offered revenge on a silver platter and plan to off him in the end." Meadow shook her head slowly. "That's a risky proposition. If Silas and Des turn on Van, it's possible the Bianco family will hunt them for blood."

"This is twisted." Ian exhaled loudly.

It was. "Either way, Van Moore and possibly the Biancos are involved." Which meant they still had hope of locating Brooke. "Isla, find me—"

"I'm two steps ahead of you." When Meadow's phone pinged with an incoming email, Isla grinned. "I've sent a list of properties owned by the Biancos' known shell corps. Two of the addresses are properties they've bought in the past month near Cattle Bend, a mining company and a warehouse."

A charge of *knowing* zipped through Meadow. The other sites they had been surveilling had come up empty. Given this new information about the Bianco family's involvement, it was obvious to everyone involved. Most likely, Brooke was going to be in one of those two places.

Ian knew it, too. He looked at her above the phone, his expression resolute. There was no way he was going to go quietly to the safe house now.

"You're the best, Isla." Meadow blew a kiss at the phone. "When I get back, you're getting coffee and a long conversation."

A shadow crossed Isla's face. "I'm going to need that conversation."

They might be sitting on a ticking time bomb, but something was going on with Isla, and it was more than the anonymous tip that had ruined her chance to foster a baby. Meadow looked at Ian, who'd paused halfway to the door. "Has something else happened to you, Isla?"

"It's nothing."

"Isla…"

"Fine." Isla glanced away from the camera and then back again. "There's nothing to be done about it now, but someone called my bank and impersonated me. Told them I'd lost my wallet and needed all of my cards canceled and my accounts put on hold."

"Isla, no." This was the last thing she needed. "Who would do this to you?"

"I don't know. And look, it's a nuisance and nothing near as big as what you've got happening right now. Don't worry about me. It'll be fine." She offered a thin smile. "I've got a few other angles I can work, maybe see if they're communicating on any dark-web sites. Let me know if you need anything else. I'm all in on helping you shut this ring down."

Before Meadow could respond, the call ended.

The foster process weighed heavily on her friend, and now all of these strange attacks kept hitting her. Meadow would have to make sure to keep that promise of quality time with Isla when she made it back to headquarters. Although the team was close-knit, it wouldn't hurt for Isla to have all of them as listening ears.

But for now, there was a more dangerous situation at play. Meadow turned to Ian, but he was already heading out the door.

He motioned for her to follow. "Let's move."

"Slow your roll, McQueen." Rushing into the unknown would get them nowhere but dead. "We'll be wheels up as soon as I lay some groundwork. We'll have some unmarked local law enforcement cruise by to scout one location, and we'll take the other so we can hit them both at once. I want Rocco with us, and I want backup. There's no telling what we're getting into. Besides…" She walked to the window and looked through. "I think we can get some added intel by working the Des angle against Van. And I think our weak link on the inside is Des. We might be able to leverage that."

If they could, it might get them through this night without one of them getting killed.

FOURTEEN

Van Moore hadn't cracked.

As darkness fell, Meadow navigated toward an abandoned coal-mining operation about half an hour outside of town, watching the sky fade to black. It had taken several eternally long hours to put all of the pieces into play. Surveillance had revealed activity in the old mine shaft, and while one team of law enforcement officers from various agencies headed there with Meadow, Rocco and Ian, another team moved on a warehouse between Cattle Bend and Missoula. While it appeared to be empty, they didn't want to take any chances.

Ian rode silently in the passenger seat while Rocco manned a laptop in the back, keeping track of the moving pieces and waiting to see if either Des or Silas powered up their cell phones, giving away their location. They'd been dark since Brooke's kidnapping.

No one had spoken outside of a few updates from Rocco about team positions and ETAs. They were on their own, headed to meet the special response team from the state highway patrol and federal agents from Missoula. In half an hour, this should all be over.

Hopefully without having to involve the coroner.

Meadow shook off the thought and laid a hand on Ian's wrist. "You doing okay over there?"

In the rearview, Rocco looked up with mild interest, his face lit by the laptop screen.

Okay, he'd seen her touch Ian. So what? She shouldn't, but she couldn't help it. He was hurting. She wanted to fix it.

She'd always wanted to fix his hurts.

There had been a wounded air about him from the moment she'd met him. The more they'd worked together, the more she'd fallen for him. He claimed he wasn't one who got close to people, but he'd reached out to her on more than one occasion. Had shared his thoughts and cracked jokes that made her laugh until she cried. He'd had a reckless attitude about him when he first went undercover, a half-wild manner that had made her wonder if he cared whether he lived or died.

Until that bullet had almost ripped him from this world. In the hospital, she'd recognized the fight in him. He had a will to live. She didn't know where he'd found it, but he'd found it.

He'd seemed relieved to see her at his bedside when he awoke after the shooting. And he'd spoken more about God lately, though it seemed like a distant relationship.

At least it was something more than he'd had before. She prayed he'd eventually realize how much God loved him.

Maybe then, he'd realize other people loved him, too.

Ian shrugged away and turned to look at Rocco. "What's our ETA? And is the rest of the team in place?"

Nothing had changed in the three minutes since Rocco had last given an update, but Meadow heard the purpose behind the question loud and clear… Ian wanted to focus on the job ahead, not get tangled up in thinking about her.

Message received, and rightly so.

Meadow moved her hand to the steering wheel while Rocco answered as though he hadn't just handed out that info. "The team is in place and waiting for us to arrive. Meadow will act as team leader. We're about eight minutes out."

Ian was going to feel every one of those eight minutes keenly.

He nodded. "Any sure sign of Brooke or the others?"

"Negative. But they are reporting movement in the mine shaft. The other team says their location is silent. No one seems to be— Hang on." Rocco pressed his earbud deeper into his ear, listening. "Pull over. I'm transferring this call to the car's speakers."

Ian and Meadow locked eyes as she pulled to the side of the narrow back road, moving the tires from the edge of the pavement as far as she dared.

By the time she shifted into Park, Isla's voice was coming through the speakers. "You're headed into an ambush. I've notified the team already. They're pulling back. Silas has a bunch of local muscle waiting to slaughter anyone who gets near that mine shaft."

Ian pounded his knees and stared out the side window, the air around him practically humming with tension.

"But…" Isla rushed ahead before Meadow could react. "I think I know where they are."

"Where?" Ian whirled toward the speaker as though Isla could see him. "Give us something. Anything."

"O-okay," Isla stuttered, likely shocked at the sound of an unknown person spouting orders. She took it in stride, responding as though Ian had a right to demand answers from her. "You guys need to turn around and head to the address I'm texting to Rocco. I've got backup headed your way, but given how thin you guys are spread and the direction you're heading, you'll probably beat them there."

"Got it. Putting it into GPS. It's twelve miles in the direction we just came from, at an old truck stop by the highway." Rocco was fully focused. "Isla, how confident are you about this?"

"I'll give you a 95 percent chance of finding Brooke and a couple of others there, but you have to hurry."

Hanging a U-turn, Meadow roared toward town, pushing the limits on the SUV. If Isla said they would find Brooke there, she trusted her. Still, what were they getting into? "Where did you get your intel?"

"Short version? Des and Van have been communicating on the dark web. I managed to crack a direct message thread between the two of them. Turns out, Van knew Des was alive the entire time. They've been communicating for years, and she was even bold enough to visit him in prison several times. Their plan is to get the pipeline set up then take down Silas, all the while making Silas think *he's* the one working with Van behind Des's back. Des and Van will run the Bianco family's new Western operations, while the rest of the family maintains the Eastern arm. Guys, this text stream is a gold mine. I've got enough to take everyone down, including the Biancos. Finally."

While that was certainly good news, this was worse than Meadow had ever imagined. It was sick on a thousand levels. "So Des double-crossed Van, he went to prison, but they're still working together?"

"Girl, based on some of these messages, they're more than working together. They give me the ick."

"So how do you know where we're headed is the right place?" Ian gripped the handle above the door, hanging on as Meadow took the curves faster than safety dictated. Hopefully, the K-9s were hanging tough in the cargo area.

"They talked openly in these messages about buying this one property under a different identity. It's separate from both the Bianco shell corp and the Thornton shell corp in order to prevent Silas from finding out about it. Des is there with three victims, one of which is Brooke."

"They really did get candid in those texts."

"They didn't see me coming, that's for sure. They thought they were safe to say whatever they wanted. Des talked Silas into setting you up for an ambush at the mine shaft. He thinks Des has the girls at one of the Thornton stash houses. He's at the mine, ready to exact the revenge he believes Des set up for him. The real plan is to take Ian down and to kill Silas in the cross fire. But, guys? You need to hurry. They plan to move these victims within the hour whether Van is there or not. They've built in all sorts of contingencies."

"So why did Van come at me today? It got him caught."

"Not sure. Looks like he simply saw a chance and took it, maybe planning to take you to Silas then kill both of you without all of this drama. I do know they overheard Brooke talking at the diner, and taking her was a way to get you involved. Silas is consumed with revenge, and Des is exploiting that to keep him from figuring out what's really going on."

This was a twisted path none of them had seen coming. "Isla, you're a rock star. Never leave us." She'd just saved their lives and the lives of the captives at the truck stop.

"Just doing my job." There was an undercurrent in the words that likely had everything to do with the personal stress she was under. When she glanced in the rearview, it was clear Rocco had heard it, too. "I'll inform the other team you're on the way. You'll have to park in a wooded area about a quarter of a mile before the truck stop to avoid detection. I've highlighted the area on a map I sent to Rocco. Check in soon. Be safe."

"Unless forced, we won't go in without backup. Thanks again, Isla."

None of them spoke as Meadow wound through the back roads, following Rocco's directions as she headed for the wooded area near the truck stop.

Once there, Meadow located a narrow trail that led into the woods, killed the lights and pulled the SUV in. Quickly, they geared up in their bulletproof vests, including one borrowed for Ian from the Cattle Bend PD. They checked their weapons and leashed the K-9s. Meadow grabbed the small bag that held Brooke's sweater then they made their way along the edge of the wood line, navigating by moonlight.

The moon was a blessing and a curse, lighting their way but making their shapes and shadows obvious to anyone watching for them.

Hopefully, no one was on the lookout. If Silas and Des believed their ambush plan was working, they'd be focused on the mine. Des wouldn't be concerned about a location she believed was entirely secret.

Please, God, let it be so.

The roar of cars zipping along the highway grew louder as they neared the clearing where the abandoned truck stop stood. The woods ran right up to the concrete parking pad. Weeds grew between cracks in the broken and uneven surface. That would make it difficult to move quickly. One bad step could break an ankle or take a person to the ground.

The building itself was silent, the windows boarded up long ago, which kept them from seeing inside.

It also kept whoever was inside from seeing out.

Ian tapped Meadow's shoulder, then pointed.

At the edge of the front window, a thin sliver of light shone. Someone was definitely in the broken-down square red building.

Keeping to the edge of the trees, they moved toward the rear of the building. A sedan that matched the description of the one involved in Brooke's kidnapping was tucked behind an old car wash. Inside, a box truck sat with its engine running. It would be invisible from the road, blocked from view by the main building.

Meadow exhaled through pursed lips, releasing the dread and relief that tried to clamp down on her heart. They were nearly too late...but they'd made it. Now wasn't the time to let emotion take control. Now was the time to be tactical and methodical.

She backed into the cover of the trees and addressed her small team. "I'm going to take Grace around and see if she picks up Brooke's scent at the car, just to be sure. Beyond that, we'll wait for the team to arrive."

Ian straightened, moon shadows doing nothing to soften his tense features. "But—"

"Racing in alone and blind could get everyone killed."

Rocco looked toward the building. "Cocoa and I will see if we can gather any useful intel. How many players are inside, where Brooke and the others are. Once the team gets here, we can move in."

The plan was dangerous but necessary. "Just be sure to—"

A crash and a scream shattered the stillness. A female ran from the rear of the building, racing toward the highway.

A gunshot cracked and the figure dropped to the ground. Motionless.

Gunfire.

Bullets.

A body lying motionless in a parking lot.

Ian jerked as though an invisible force grabbed him by the neck and snatched him backward in time. As the gunfire echoed, memories rushed forward, layering over the present until he wasn't sure if he was the victim or the witness.

But as the sound died away, the memory died with it.

Clarity returned in a rush as shocking as the gunshot.

That could be Brooke.

This wasn't about him. This was about her. About his makeshift team.

There were only three of them against an unknown foe, and he couldn't let them down. If he did, one of them could die.

Meadow could die.

The thought shifted his heart into overdrive and fired fear into the deepest reaches of his mind. He went emotionally numb, something he'd only experienced on a handful of occasions in the heat of overseas combat.

Meadow was already on the move. "We can't wait. We have to go in." She looked back. "Rocco, take the front as planned. I'll go for the girl. Ian, cover me from the rear of the prop—"

"I'll go for the girl." He was already in motion, weapon drawn. "It might be Brooke." Meadow had to understand what drove him. His cousin might need him, and come death or life, he was going to be there for her. She was the only one who'd ever loved him for who he was.

Except, possibly, Meadow.

She hesitated, watching him. Time seemed to slow, and she moved to say something, her hand hovering in the space between them.

But the moment passed. She drew her sidearm and headed toward the rear of the property. "I'm going to disable the truck, then I'll have your back. Don't move until you hear the engine stop." She looked at him, her face in shadow. "Be careful. You'll be in—" Her expression turned to worry before she reset it to a hard-core law enforcement mask.

Still, her unspoken words rattled in his skull. *You'll be in the cross fire.*

No doubt. Once that engine stopped running, whoever was inside might be alerted to their presence. If the bullets started flying, he'd be between Meadow and Des.

But that couldn't stop him. He'd been living for himself for years, driven first by the belief his life didn't matter, then by the fire of fear.

Fear for himself had driven him away.

Fear for his cousin had brought him back.

It was time to step up and reclaim who he was born to be. One of the cowboys at the rodeo had said everyone was formed with a purpose. They were all here for a reason.

Maybe it was time to believe it.

Lord, keep us safe. Get us out of this alive. And whoever that girl is, let her be okay. He couldn't bring himself to accept it might be Brooke bleeding on pavement still hot from the earlier July sun.

To the right, metal squeaked. Half a minute passed, maybe more, then the hum of the truck's engine died.

Now or never.

No shadows covered his approach across the open pavement, so he stayed as close to the center of the building's side as he could. That should keep him largely out of sight of the doors at the front and rear until he was in position.

At the corner of the building, he pressed his back against faded red cinder blocks and caught his breath. He needed to be steady to get that girl out of this alive.

Holding his Sig at the ready, he peeked around the rear of the building, first at where the door should be, then at the person on the ground.

She was moving, dragging herself slowly toward the woods, heading in his direction. She was forty feet away, and if the person who shot her returned, they'd have Ian squarely in their crosshairs.

If he wanted to save her, then he had no choice but to give away his position.

Looking toward the van, he tried to get a high sign from Meadow, but he couldn't see her.

He was on his own. Where was their backup?

Fear tried to worm its way up his throat. It squirmed in his chest and threatened to choke him. Breathing deeply, focusing on the struggling woman, he said another quick prayer. Only God could get them out of this.

Ian couldn't let her die, and that was exactly what would happen if he didn't find the strength to move.

Before fear could get a tighter toehold, he rounded the corner, sticking close to the wall, trying to keep his breaths from racing out of control.

The rear door of the building was closed. The windows were boarded up. If he moved quickly, he might be able to save them both.

With one final prayer, he raced forward and dropped beside the girl.

She'd stopped moving, lying cheek-down on the pavement. Light brown hair spilled around her, matted with blood.

It wasn't Brooke, but that brought little relief. This young woman was injured. Somewhere behind those thick concrete walls, his cousin was still a prisoner.

But before he could rescue Brooke, he had to get this victim to safety.

Ian glanced at the door, then back to her. He laid his fingers at her throat and found a thready pulse, then shook her gently. "Hey." He leaned close to her ear and whispered, "Can you walk? I'm here to help."

Nothing.

He'd have to carry her.

Closing his eyes, he tucked his gun into its holster, fighting a wave of panic. If someone came out the door while he was carrying an unconscious woman, he'd be unable to reach for his weapon—

No.

He had to trust Meadow and Rocco were out there and had his back. He had to trust the things he'd heard about God over the past two years. That verse Hayden had on his chaps, the one about God knowing his days.

He was important. Known. Loved.

He had a purpose.

Maybe it was to save this girl at the expense of his own life.

Maybe it wasn't.

But in this moment, there was no denying the call that was directly in front of him.

Quickly, he rolled the girl over and scanned her for wounds in the moonlight. Blood seeped from her shoulder. She was likely in shock.

A firefighter's carry was out. He could hurt her worse. Instead, he cradled her against his chest and jogged toward the shelter of the trees.

He made it to the corner of the building before the girl stirred and jerked.

Then screamed.

"Shh… Shh…" Ian fought to hold her as she struggled. There was no way to quiet her, nothing he could do to silence her panicked shrieks. "I'm here to help."

Still, she fought and wailed.

He rounded the corner of the building as the back door squeaked open. Footsteps crunched on gravel slowly at first then faster, following the cries of the young woman in his arms.

In seconds, they'd be dead.

She screamed again, but the sound died abruptly as though

the volume had been cut. She went limp in his arms. Still breathing, still moving, but she'd apparently exhausted her oxygen.

He leaned forward, preparing to settle her to the ground. Maybe he could draw his weapon and—

Footsteps beside him. He whipped around as quickly as he could with the weight of the girl in his arms.

Rocco approached with Cocoa at his side. "Thought you could use a bodyguard."

"Dude, am I glad to see you." Other than Meadow at his hospital bedside and in the woods just a couple of days ago, he'd never been more relieved to see another human being. "She's alive. Looks like a shoulder wound. Probably going into shock. What's our situation?"

Two gunshots echoed. Tough to tell if they came from the building or the trees.

Ian jumped and almost dropped the woman.

Someone cursed, and the back door slammed. The shots must have been cover fire from Meadow.

Ian nearly collapsed in relief.

Rocco reached for the young woman. "We're directly under a cell tower, so no service. No idea where backup is. We're out of time. I'll take her. You get inside. I saw two young women through the crack between the board and the window, and one of them looks like the girl in the photo of Brooke. Both are alive. Didn't see any extra guards, but that's not much help. We've made our presence known. Also, watch yourself. Cocoa alerted to an accelerant, though it could be old from the time when this place was an active truck stop."

So they were battling guns and the threat of fire, and they'd lost the element of surprise. Those women were in more danger now than ever before.

Ian passed the young woman to Rocco, who headed for the relative safety of the woods with Cocoa close behind.

Ian moved toward the front, urgency pushing him forward. If they didn't move quickly, Brooke and the other girl would be dead as soon as Des could pull the trigger.

Ian crept along the wall and peeked around the front of the building.

Nothing moved in the moonlight. With the wide parking lot to the front and the highway to the other side, there were few places for a sniper to hide.

That didn't mean there wasn't one, but if there was, he'd have taken out Rocco. Entering from the front was likely their safest bet.

Ian ducked below the window level and passed the glass double front door. Though the glass on one side was cracked, the doors were chained and locked, then boarded up from the inside. No good entry point there.

At the far window, he crouched by the thin gap between the wood and cinder block and peered inside, searching the sliver of room he was able to see.

The part of the old convenience store that was visible was filthy, littered with trash and layered with years of moisture and grime. The light was dim and flickery, emanating from an old oil camping lantern on a shelf that probably once held snack food.

No sign of Brooke.

Shifting to the left, he tried another angle.

There.

Bile rose in the back of his throat.

In the old refrigerated units along the back wall, Brooke and another girl were imprisoned behind grimy glass doors, huddled in the space where sodas and beer used to be displayed. It was like a sick museum piece, a prison on display.

One door hung open, likely where the third woman had been imprisoned. Des had probably been moving her to the truck when she broke away.

Des was nowhere to be seen, but that didn't mean she wasn't on her way in to murder her prisoners. He had to move, even without backup.

If only he could signal to Brooke he was nearby, but she was curled into a ball, her arms wrapped around her legs and her chin resting on her knees as she stared blankly at the refrigerator door.

Reluctantly, Ian moved to the front doors, inspecting them. There was no way to break the heavy chains, but the boards behind the glass appeared to be plywood, and the doors themselves had not weathered well. If he could shatter the glass that was already damaged, he might be able to kick the plywood away from the wall.

It would take several blows and possibly a gunshot. Would he be able to breach before the noise brought Des running?

Did he have any other choice?

Backing away to avoid ricochet, he lifted his pistol, aimed at the corner of the cracked door...

And fired.

FIFTEEN

*C*rack!

Meadow jumped as a gunshot rang out from the front of the building. Grace had just alerted to Brooke's scent, and now she watched Meadow, anticipating a treat that wasn't coming.

Crack! Crack! Crack!

Three more pops in rapid succession. A series of hollow thuds followed.

Meadow motioned for Grace to heel then peered around the back of the box truck. She couldn't see what was happening. Rocco and Cocoa were entering the woods with the girl, which meant Ian had moved to the front of the building.

Beyond that, she was in the dark. Literally.

She needed to do something.

Either those gunshots meant Des had done the unthinkable, or Ian was creating a distraction so Meadow could approach.

Whichever it was, she had to move now.

With one last scan of the area, Meadow rushed around the vehicle toward the open space between the car wash and the main building with Grace beside her. There was nowhere to hide and no time to take it slow. This was what she trained for, what she had prepared to do for her entire career...

Put herself and her partner in the line of fire to save another person.

Tensed against a potential bullet, she charged into the fray.

The bullet never came. She ran until she hit the back of the building, taking only a moment to catch her breath and to check on Grace before she eased along the warm cinderblock wall to the door.

In her rush to defend the front, Des had left it unlocked.

Either that, or this was a trap. They'd assumed Des was alone. They could be dead wrong.

Motioning for Grace to sit, Meadow allowed her partner to sniff the sweater once again, then commanded her to investigate the door.

Immediately, Grace sat and looked up at Meadow, waiting to receive a treat for a successful search.

Brooke was inside.

With a quick pat to Grace's head, she passed on a small treat.

Standing to the hinge side of the door, Meadow readied her pistol then extended her arm, pulling the door open with the other.

Two gunshots sounded.

She flinched, but the shots hadn't been aimed at her and Grace. They came from the front of the building.

Another thud reverberated in the building. Another gunshot rang out.

Pulling in a deep breath and releasing it slowly, Meadow steadied herself and stepped into the room, gaze sweeping from left to right as Grace trotted beside her.

The storage room was lit by flickering overhead fluorescent light. It was empty save for several broken shelves that held old tools, ancient auto fluids and discarded parts. A tiny bathroom on the right stood empty.

She hurried to the door in the center of the wall, nestled between shelves. She was in a fatal funnel with nowhere for her and Grace to take cover as they advanced.

Stepping into a short hallway with a closed door on each side, she paused, looking straight through to the front door. Another thud, and the wood at one side of the door cracked, the plywood sheet falling crookedly.

Two more gunshots, this time from the inside. Two bullets splintered the wood.

Ian was coming in, and Des was determined to stop him.

Ian would never survive, and he had to know that, yet he was doing what it took to rescue his cousin. He would be exposed if he came through that door, wide-open to the line of fire.

The advantage belonged to Des…

But Des didn't know about Meadow.

Creeping to the door, Meadow peeked into the storefront.

Des had concealed herself behind the counter, gun at the ready, less than six feet away.

Meadow had to move before Ian came through the door and sacrificed his life. One quick prayer. One deep breath. "Federal agent!" She stepped into the room, Glock leveled at Des. "Put down the weapon!"

Rolling to a seated position, Des fired as Meadow's finger squeezed the trigger.

Indescribable force slammed into Meadow's chest, blowing the air from her lungs and staggering her backward. She hit the doorjamb and dropped to her knees, clawing at her chest, trying to make her lungs expand. Gasping. Suffocating.

A guttural cry tore the air. Hers? Someone else's?

Other screams blended with the ringing in her ears in a horrifying symphony.

More gunshots. An explosion. Shrieks. Shouts.

Grace shoved her nose against Meadow's face, whimpering.

Meadow tried to jerk her head away as she dug at the pressure in her chest, desperate for air.

"Meadow!"

The sound of Ian's voice jolted through her and she gasped, allowing her lungs to fill. On hands and knees, she heaved in air, fighting through pain to get the oxygen she needed.

Was that…smoke? Was it real or was she hallucinating?

She inhaled again, her throat burning.

The smoke was real.

Clarity rushed in. *Des.*

Des's shot hit her in the vest. She had to defend herself. To defend Ian. Where was her gun?

There. She reached for it, but feet appeared between her and the weapon. She tried to come up swinging, but the pain in her chest was too great.

And then…Ian. He lifted her chin. "Look at me, Meadow. Can you get up? I need you with me."

She nodded, the sight of him clicking reality into place. Her breath was constricted, but at least she could focus. "Des. She…"

"She's no longer a threat, but her second shot went wild. Hit the lantern. We have to move. To get the girls out. Now."

Calling on every reserve she had, Meadow grabbed Ian's hand and let him pull her up. Her eyes stung as smoke thickened the air.

Grace took her place by Meadow's leg, watching and waiting for the next command. Her partner was brave and undeterred by the danger.

Fire licked the walls at the front of the building, feeding on trash, dry wood and discarded containers of auto fluids.

The sight and smell propelled Meadow forward despite her pain and breathlessness. "Where are—" Her head spun. Two young women, locked behind glass. They banged the doors of the old refrigeration unit, screaming, crying. *The girls.*

Thick chains woven between the handles secured them inside.

Meadow turned quickly, her vision whirling from pain and fumes. This was more than simply smoke. Something chemical was on fire. There was no telling what they were inhaling. Her eyes watered and her lungs burned with the stench and the smoke. The room wobbled, and her already labored breaths grew shallow.

Ian grabbed her arm. "Stay with me, Meadow."

She was trying. Oh, she was trying. But the darkness was closing in.

Sensing Meadow's distress, Grace leaned against her leg, pressing in tightly as though she could support her.

Meadow hardly felt it. She stared at the frantic young women, trying to form a plan. They couldn't shoot the glass, not without a risk of ricochet hitting the captives or themselves. Double-pane glass was a beast to break without something to concentrate the blow.

"We need something sharp." Ian looked frantically around the room, but the smoke was thickening.

Something sharp.

The tools in the back room.

Meadow stumbled, righted herself and wrestled pain and lack of oxygen to make her way, half doubled over, to the storage room. Grace kept nudging the back of her leg as though she was herding Meadow toward safety.

The air was clearer, but that didn't make it any easier to

breathe through the agony that seemed to splinter her side with every inhale.

She grabbed a hammer and a screwdriver and made her way into the smoke, hunched over, moving through a thick sludge of half consciousness. Holding out her offering to Ian, she sagged against the wall.

He braced the screwdriver against the bottom corner of the glass door and looked up at his cousin. "Brooke, back up as far as you can."

His shout was lost to the roar of flames and the thunder in Meadow's skull.

Ian pulled back the hammer and drove it into the screwdriver.

Glass shattered and rained onto the concrete floor.

Meadow collapsed with it as the world turned black.

Brooke flew into Ian's arms as Meadow sagged to the floor and Grace took up a protective stance by her stricken partner. The K-9 looked to Ian as though he would know what to do.

He didn't.

Like a drowning victim, Brooke clung to him, wrapping her arms tightly around him. She shook with gasping sobs driven by panic and smoke.

It ripped his heart out to pry her arms from around his neck. He placed his hands on her cheeks, forcing her to look him in the eye. "Brooke. Listen. Listen!"

His shout seemed to shatter her panic. She stood in front of him, shoulders heaving with rapid breaths, eyes wide, cheeks wet with tears.

"Good." Ian rested his palms on his cousin's cheeks and pressed a kiss to her forehead, relief coursing through him. She was safe.

But Meadow, Grace and the young woman who screamed

from the other refrigerated unit were still in danger. The room grew hotter, and smoke depleted the oxygen. "Go to the back door. Help is on the way."

Her head swung back and forth as her eyes widened with worsening panic. She moved her lips as though she wanted to protest.

"You can do this. You're strong. I know you can. I have to get the others out."

With a gasping breath, Brooke finally nodded, her damp cheeks slipping beneath his palms.

Sirens screamed through the roar of the flames. Squealing tires and racing engines were barely audible. "Help's here. Go to them. You're safe. I'll be out before you know it."

And if he wasn't, she'd always know he'd loved her enough to return for her.

One more hesitation, then Brooke pulled away, disappearing into the back room, hopefully headed for freedom.

Bending to retrieve the screwdriver and the hammer, Ian gulped cooler air near the floor, refusing to look at Meadow where she'd heaped to the concrete.

Grace stood guard, barking as though Ian didn't understand the urgency.

He more than understood. If he looked at her, though, he'd lose focus. Whatever was wrong with her, he couldn't help until he freed the other young woman. His heart and mind balked at the idea of turning his back on Meadow, even for a moment, but he inhaled one more burst of relatively smoke-free air and moved to the next refrigerated unit.

The woman inside had already slid into the far corner, huddled on the slimy floor with her head bent over her knees. Either she'd heard Ian's earlier instructions to Brooke, or she'd given up hope and was waiting to die.

Wedging the screwdriver against the corner of the glass, Ian pulled the hammer back and drove it toward the handle.

The flickering light from the fire and the eye-watering smoke and fumes threw his aim off. He smacked the door. The hammer bounced off the glass, cracking him on the hand that held the screwdriver.

Wincing, he bit back a cry. He had to free this prisoner. Had to move fast. Had to get to Meadow.

With a roar from deep inside his chest, he smashed the hammer against the screwdriver handle.

The window cracked but didn't shatter.

Abandoning the screwdriver, Ian dropped to his hands and knees seeking cleaner air and better sight. He pounded the cracked window with the hammer until the glass shattered, falling around him like crystal rain.

The young woman scrambled to her feet and shoved Ian to the side, bolting toward the flames, frantic to be free.

"No!" Ian leaped to his feet and grabbed the panicked woman around the waist. He hauled her against him. "No! You have to get out. You can't go that way. You're free now. I'm going to get you to somewhere safe!"

She fought, kicking and screaming and crying, hysterical and likely unable to even hear him.

He couldn't release her to attend to Meadow. She might run headlong into the flames.

No, he'd have to carry her to safety, leaving Meadow behind.

Could he?

His heart shattered like that glass.

The girl wrestled and struggled, landing an elbow to Ian's ribs so sharply he almost dropped her.

The pain galvanized him into action. Lifting her feet from the floor, he carried the panicked woman into the dark storage room and sat her feet onto the floor, shoving her toward the exterior door and freedom. "Run! Get out of here!"

She stumbled, looked back at him with a stricken expression, then raced through the rear storage room and out into the night, where red, white and blue flashes of light indicated help had arrived.

He didn't take time to feel relief. Instead, he turned back to rescue Meadow.

The smoke was thicker than ever, the acrid chemical odor overwhelming. Dropping to his hands and knees, he crawled toward the refrigerators, feeling his way along the floor as the smoke filled the room.

Grace appeared in the flickering darkness, licking his face and tugging at his sleeve, urging him forward.

A hand appeared on the concrete before him.

Meadow's hand.

As his breaths labored, he wrapped his fingers around her wrist and backed away, then tugged her limp body toward him. He didn't dare stand and pick her up. They'd both suffocate.

Dirt and grit dug into his jeans as he scooted back a few more feet and dragged her with him.

Grace kept a slow pace and barked an alert that sounded more like a command to keep moving.

Lord, let her be alive. Let her make it through this. You got Brooke out of here, get us out of here. Please.

The prayer looped in his head, sincere in its repetition. Over and over he tugged, the faint feel of her pulse tapping unevenly against his palm.

The room was unbearably hot. The inches were hard-won, and her lifeless weight grew heavier as lack of oxygen drained his strength.

Please, God. He tugged again, her wrist slipping in his

sweat-soaked palms. *Please. Don't let me realize I love her just to lose her.*

He did love her, and he should have told her sooner. When that had happened, he had no idea, but the emotion drove him to keep going, inch by inch, to keep pulling them both toward freedom.

He'd loved her when he saw her in the woods days ago. When he'd left for Texas and even before. The emotion had crept up on him, sneaking into his heart so stealthily, so unfamiliar, he'd failed to recognize the warmth and longing he felt toward her for what they were.

Love.

With a guttural cry, he tugged her into the storage room, but the smoke had begun to fill that space as well.

The fluorescent light flickered and died.

Grace continued to bark.

His strength was sapped. It felt as though he'd been dragging Meadow in darkness through a thick swamp of mud for years. Time was irrelevant. Space made no sense. His ears rang and his brain fogged. He had no idea if he was moving backward or forward or—

Strong hands gripped him under the arms and tugged him upward.

Meadow's wrist slipped from his grip. *No!* He tried to cry out, tried to fight, but his muscles were water. His words were gone. He was somewhere between life and death, awake and asleep.

He'd been here once before, staring up at a clear blue sky from pavement as the blood seeped from his body and his life drifted away. He'd thought of Meadow then.

Why now, when his life was leaving him again, did he suddenly remember?

Muffled sounds. His body moving on its own, bumping across the floor as a force dragged him backward.

Fresh, clean air hit his lungs. The hands moved away. He was flat on his back on the warm pavement. Staring up at the stars as they faded into darkness.

He'd been here before.

Meadow...

SIXTEEN

Everything hurt.

Literally *everything*.

Meadow's lungs burned. Her head pounded. Her arms and legs were lead. Even her eyelids fought every attempt to open them.

"Here she is." A gentle female voice spoke above her, and the light seemed to dim as someone leaned over her. "She's coming around now."

Who was this person in her...in her—where was she anyway?

When had she fallen asleep?

She managed one blink and caught a flash of bright light.

Light. Fire.

Fire. Ian.

Brooke. The other girl.

They had to get out! "Ian." His name croaked from her dry throat. Was he okay? Had she lost him again, this time forever? Tears leaked from her eyes and ran into her ears. She'd never told him—

More soft words and then another presence beside her. A hand rested on her arm. "It's me. I'm fine. We're all fine."

Ian.

Meadow turned her head toward the warmth of his hand.

"You're here." Her voice croaked. Maybe the words hadn't even come out.

"Not planning on going anywhere."

"Good." While her eyes refused to open, the corners of her mouth tipped up. "'Cause I love you."

Sleep overtook her, and the next time she awoke, it was to filtered light. Her throat was dry and her head pounded, but her brain seemed to be on line. "Where am I?"

"Hey. You're back." Ian's soft voice came from her left, and then he appeared, leaning into her field of vision. "You're at St. Patrick Hospital in Missoula. You broke some ribs and punctured a lung when Des shot your vest at close range, and you inhaled a hefty dose of all sorts of chemicals." His voice sounded as raw as hers felt. "You had a quick surgery to do some repairs, and you'll feel like a horse kicked you for a while, but you'll be fine."

Everything rushed in. The fire. The gun battle. The young women behind glass. "Help me sit up."

Ian pushed the button on her bed and raised her head until she was partially upright. The pain as her ribs shifted was dull, but that was likely due to whatever was dripping from the IV bag by her head.

Ian helped her sip from a cup of the sweetest, coolest water she'd ever tasted. It slipped down her raw throat like balm, giving strength to her voice. "Brooke and the others? And what about her friend, the one she was worried about?"

He set the cup aside. "Brooke's fine. She's up the hall with…with her mother and will be released tomorrow. The other woman, Trinity James, is in a room with her parents. Cassidy Michaels was the shooting victim. She took a hit to the shoulder but came out of surgery and will recover after physical therapy. Once Van figured out there was no hope for him unless he cut a deal, he gave up the location of the remaining missing persons, and they're being reunited with their families as we speak. Her friend is safe as well. Silas, Des and Van got so wrapped up in taking out their revenge on me that they never pursued a meeting with her."

She couldn't have asked for a happier ending. "And Grace?"

"Chilling with Rocco at your place."

Tension leaked from her shoulders. Until it released, she hadn't even realized she'd been carrying it. The girls were safe. Her partner was safe. "Des? Silas? Their crew?"

"Des won't threaten anyone anymore." He glanced away then back to her. "Silas and the three hired guns he had with him were picked up at the mining shaft. Based on the intel your friend Isla uncovered, an operation has been set into motion against the Bianco organization. We did a lot of good in the past couple of days."

"And nearly died doing it." Ian had to have faced his worst nightmare, with guns blasting and fire raging. It felt good just to be in his presence, to see he was alive and okay. "How about you? How are you?"

"I'm good. Scratchy throat. Sore chest. I fared better than you did."

"I meant how are you in here?" She lifted her hand, partially tethered by the IV, and touched his temple, then let her palm slide to his cheek. "You've had a rough few days."

He grasped her hand and lowered it to the bed, carefully twining his fingers with hers. He smiled as he stared at their hands, his thumb running up and down the side of hers to create all kinds of warm fuzzies that defied the painkillers coursing through her body.

She could certainly feel the things he wasn't saying. "I'm doing pretty okay. I mean, I'm a long way from being totally fine, but I think I see a path in that direction. I finally realized it's not about me. I was willing to…to face Des's bullets to rescue someone else, someone I care about." He shifted his gaze to hers. "Two people I care about."

"You laid down your life for your friends." It was like the Bible verse said. That was the greatest love, and Ian had found it. Hopefully, he realized the verse applied to him, too. That Jesus had laid down His life for Ian.

"For my cousin." He held her gaze. "For you. You're more than my friend, Meadow. And…" His soft smile morphed into a mischievous grin. "From what you said when you were still a little loopy, I think you'd agree."

"What?" Grogginess blew away. Meadow tried to sit taller, but she couldn't. What did he know? What had she said under the effects of painkillers and anesthesia? Pulling her hand from his, she raised the bed until she was almost eye to eye with him. "What? Ian…" She put all of the threat she could muster into her voice. "What did I say?"

He leaned closer, resting his lips against her ear. "That you love me."

Her eyes slipped closed. Maybe if she tried really hard, she could find what little bit of anesthesia was coursing through her and slip back into unconsciousness. Maybe when she woke up, she'd be back in time somewhere before she'd let that slip.

Ian wasn't a guy who wanted love. He wasn't a guy who believed he was worthy of it. If he thought she was in love with him, he'd bolt.

Except…he hadn't.

When she opened her eyes, he drew back slightly so she could see his eyes. For the longest time, he simply scanned her face as though he could lock this moment in his heart forever.

Either that or he was looking for a gentle way to let her down. She'd backtrack, save him the trouble. "Look, I—"

"I love you, too, Meadow Ames." Leaning forward, he pressed a gentle kiss to her forehead, his voice a low whisper. "That's all you get from me until we're out of here and can talk somewhere more private, like a spider-infested bunker."

All of her emotions choked on a chuckle. This was Ian. The man she loved. The one who apparently loved her back. He was not going to dive headlong into the mushy and the gushy.

At least, not yet. She had a feeling it lived inside of him somewhere, though. It was going to be fun bringing that out. "About those spiders, Carpenter. I'm not sure I love you that much."

"Keep insulting me, and I'll go live in that bunker."

When he started to back away, she laid a hand on the back of his neck and pulled him close, pressing a kiss to his forehead. "Only if you take me with you."

"I think I can do better than a—"

"Yuck and gag and ick and all of that stuff." Rocco's voice from the door cut short any further *mushy and gushy*. "It took you guys long enough, but seriously, it can wait."

"You're an uninvited guest, Roc. You can leave just as easily as you arrived." Meadow tapped her forehead against Ian's then dropped her hand as he sat back in the chair.

Rocco stepped into the room, his smile betraying his words. Walking over to stand beside Ian, he looked down at Meadow. "I hear you're going to survive."

"Yeah. You can't lay claim to my gourmet kitchen just yet."

"Such a waste on you." He bumped a knuckle against her shoulder, sobering. "Glad you're okay, M." Clearing his throat, he backed away and studied her IV. "How would you feel about putting a nice *pomodoro* sauce in this thing? See if we can give you Italian blood?"

Ian pretended to gag, and Meadow winced. "That's disgusting. Where's Grace?"

"In my SUV with Cocoa."

They'd be fine there, with the dedicated AC unit, built-in water bowls and alarms that alerted their phones in case of emergency.

Meadow ached to see her partner, but she wouldn't push it by asking for her in the hospital. "Hey, Roc, speaking of food, I won't deny you if you want to cook me a big ol' Italian meal when I get out of here."

Rocco settled on the bed by her feet and thumped her shin. "I would love to. Your kitchen is..." He offered an exaggerated chef's kiss then grew serious. "I'll have something ready tomorrow when you get home, but then I'm out the door."

"Why?" Meadow managed to sit up slightly, although the move cost her. "Did we find the Rocky Mountain Killer?" Her gut sank, horrid thoughts blending with the slight nausea she was already feeling. "Did he strike again?"

"No." Rocco's demeanor crumbled. Something was wrong. "Chase wants me in Elk Valley. I know the place and the people well, so he's asked me to come back."

"Why? What's wrong?" With a quick glance at Ian, Meadow held her hand out to Rocco. Something was bothering him. Could it be...? "Is there news about Cowgirl?" If their calculations were correct, the missing therapy dog had likely given birth already. What would a murderer like the RMK do to Cowgirl and her pups?

Rocco shook his head. "No word."

Her stomach sank. "Your family? Are they okay? Is it about your dad?" Rocco still grieved his father and believed the stress of the unsolved RMK case had driven him to an early grave.

"Everybody's fine." Pulling his hand away, he stared at his feet. "We have another potential suspect. Ryan York. His sister Shelley died by suicide after Seth Jenkins, our first victim, broke up with her."

Another suspect was good news, but Rocco wasn't acting like himself. Something was wrong. "So Ryan might be seeking revenge?"

"Possibly. He left Elk Valley shortly after the initial murders, so Isla is tracking him down. Preliminary info says he's got a Glock 17 registered to his name and get this... he's tall and blond."

Her heart kicked up a notch. Did they finally have a decent lead? "Tattoos?"

"Not at the time he left town, but now? Who knows?" Rocco dragged his hand through his hair. "It's a thin lead, though. He's got motive for Seth's death, but he wasn't affiliated with the YRC, so why kill the others? And why now?" Something more haunted his expression.

His pain was so palpable, Meadow wanted to hug him. When one of her teammates hurt, so did she.

He was likely thinking of his father, who'd investigated the case originally and had died with the killer still at large. Rocco had always attributed his father's heart attack to the stress of the unsolved murders, and he sought to bring closure to the work his dad had started. "Roc, you okay? I can be out the door as soon as they release me." She needed to be of use, to help her team wrap this thing up.

"Chase would never let me hear the end of it. You've been ordered to take leave, rest up." He offered a weak smile. "And I'm fine. It's just that the town's on edge, struggling with the murders. It's opened a lot of wounds and brought in a lot of fear. And now…they think the fire that killed the baseball coach was arson."

The adrenaline surge she'd felt at the news of a new suspect crashed. "Roc, no. Why?"

"Because there was another fire that killed the owner of a feed store. Both were deliberately set. Both are being investigated as homicides."

This couldn't be happening. It was heartbreaking. The last thing Elk Valley needed was more fear, more death. "I'm sorry."

"Yeah, so on top of the first serial killer, the town is dealing with a serial arsonist-slash-murderer." His gaze wandered the room. "People are scared. And you know that multiyear high-school reunion the EVHS alumni committee was planning? They've decided not to postpone it. The committee believes the town 'needs something positive to focus on.'" Rocco practically sneered.

"What?" Meadow sank against the pillow. That was utterly foolish. "Do they not understand the danger of that many people coming together all at once, many of them linked to the Young Ranchers Club and the murders?" *What are they thinking?*

"It could be our killer's dream come true."

Could a town handle so many tragedies at once? It would be a test of Elk Valley's resilience, most definitely.

"But hey!" Rocco brightened and turned his attention to Ian. "Chase said something else. Our team leader is interested in your résumé. If you're tired of the horses in Texas, he'd like to chat with you about your skills. The team could use a guy like you, and I need a good prep cook, so if you can dice onions, you're in."

Meadow scraped her teeth lightly along her dry tongue. Given Ian's trauma, Chase would likely recommend some counseling before he would be fully involved with the team, but he'd be a great fit. Ian's answer to that proposal would tell her a lot about their potential future.

He didn't look at her, focusing instead on Rocco. "Ya know…" He reached over and squeezed Meadow's fingers. "I always wanted to learn how to cook."

Ian walked up the hospital hallway, feeling more like himself than he had in years.

If he was being honest, he felt more like himself than he ever had. A clean shower and a good night's sleep in the guest bed at Meadow's home had done wonders for his mental clarity.

Knowing Brooke was safe had done wonders for his emotions.

Realizing with certainty God loved him and was holding his life in His hands had done wonders for his soul.

And a long talk with a still groggy Meadow before he'd left for the night had done wonders for his heart.

He loved her. How he'd managed to deny that truth for so many years was beyond his comprehension, but he did. She was a gift handed to him by the God who loved him more than he deserved. To know she'd loved him years ago…

Part of him regretted the time he'd spent cut off from her in WITSEC, but it had been for the best. He'd grown as a person, had drawn closer to God, had begun, even without realizing it, to love himself and to accept the love of others as he'd worked with horses as broken and wounded as he himself had been. God had been preparing him to love and be loved by a woman like Meadow.

Now that she was about to be discharged from the hospital, he was more than ready to make up for their "lost" time. Nobody knew him like she did. Nobody loved him like she did.

But someone else did love him.

Brooke.

His cousin was recovering a few doors down from Meadow, yet he hadn't seen her since he'd pulled her out of that horrible refrigeration unit. Rocco had said she was asking for him, but he hadn't been ready to run the gauntlet of his family the day before. All he'd wanted was to be with Meadow and to bask in the glow of their declared love and of the obvious love God had for both of them.

But now?

His footsteps slowed near the door to room 219. Soft voices drifted into the hall from inside.

Someone was with her. Maybe he should wait until they left.

If he did, his fragile bravery would shatter like the glass of that refrigerator door, and he'd never be able to put the pieces together again.

No, he had to go in now. To prove to his cousin she meant more to him than his fears and family pain. She needed to know he cared and she was special.

God, help me. Pulling in a deep breath and straightening his spine, he stepped into the room.

Brooke's face lit like the sunrises he'd often enjoyed over the plains in Texas. "Ian!" She stood from her perch on the edge of the bed, dressed in leggings and an oversize T-shirt, clearly about to head out the door for home.

She practically jumped on him, wrapping her arms around his neck like the exuberant toddler she used to be. "I knew you'd come! I knew you would. I asked you for help, and you came." Her voice was filled with joy, though damp tears soaked through his shirt to his shoulder.

Ian forgot everything else. This little girl…

Not a little girl anymore. In the years since he'd last seen her, she'd grown into a young lady. One who had his heart wrapped around her little finger the way a little sister would have. Holding her as she cried, knowing she was safe... Her tears of joy and relief went a long way toward healing his wounded heart.

It no longer mattered what his family believed about him. Brooke believed the best.

He sniffed back his emotion, totally unwilling to give in to tears as long as he had an audience. "Hey, I did my best."

"I knew you'd find me." Brooke backed away, swiping at her face. She looked haggard and tired, the ordeal having taken a toll, but her expression was joyful. "I never doubted it. I was telling Deputy Marshal Ames that when you came in."

Ian's gaze swung to the chair beside the bed, and the sight there sent his heart into a double thump.

Sure enough, Meadow sat straight-backed with her forehead creased in pain, though a smile lit her face. She rose slowly, standing before Ian could offer help. Waving him away, she walked to the door. "I was just chatting while Brooke's mother is getting the car. I need to go back to my room. They'll be in with my discharge papers soon, then I'll be ready to go home." She stopped long enough to kiss Ian's cheek. Far from the fire funk she'd smelled like yesterday, she now wore the scent of soap and mint and maybe even freedom, since her fondest desire was to get out of the hospital and back to Grace, who was waiting at her house with Rocco.

It was tough to pull his attention back to Brooke once Meadow exited the room.

When he did, his cousin tilted her head with a knowing grin. "You *l-o-v-e* the deputy marshal."

"Stop it." He motioned for Brooke to sit on the edge of

the bed then took the chair Meadow had vacated. "How are you doing?"

Her expression clouded. "I don't want to talk about it yet." She charged ahead before Ian could speak. "A social worker came in and let me know how to get counseling, and I'm going to do that. Right now, I just want to get out of here and..." She pulled in a long breath. "That's kind of what Meadow and I were talking about."

Meadow, not *Deputy Marshal*. Interesting.

"I'm nineteen now. I know what happens in our family. I know the things they do and..." She looked away, staring at the blank television screen. "Mom wants to talk to you, to thank you and maybe more, but she's afraid of losing her *livelihood*." The word dripped sarcasm. "She and Aunt Rena are too in love with money to stop conning people. I've put up with it for too long. Maybe someday she'll come fully around, but she's grateful to you for finding me."

Ian stared at the young woman in front of him, pained by her family's actions yet still behaving as a loving daughter. "I'm sorry you've been caught in the middle all these years."

"I chose to be, even though I was a kid. My mom is my mom, but you were always important to me." Brooke turned to him, her brown ponytail swinging over her shoulder. "I hated when you left, but now that I'm older, I see how they treated you and the position you were put into. You went out of your way to love me and to let me grieve Dean. You weren't selfish. You cared about me as a person. So many times, I wished I could have lived with you instead of them, and then you were gone. That was hard. Hearing from you again a few months ago was...good. Really good." She smiled. "And I've made a decision."

"About what?"

"I'm moving out of Mom's house. Mr. Pullman has an

apartment above the diner. He'll let me live there in exchange for me opening or closing every day. It'll free up some of his time. It's time I confronted what our family is doing, even though I still love them."

"It won't be easy." Ian's heart swelled with pride. She was taking a stand against wrong, but she was doing it in a way that respected her family as well. He could learn a few things from his younger cousin. "I'll be around now. I'm here if you need me."

"Just like always." She leaned closer, her grin full of mischief. "Maybe you'll be living near Cattle Bend?"

Ian tried not to let his face give anything away. He owed it to Meadow to talk to her first.

He stood. He should leave before his aunt returned. While he planned to reach out to his family soon to see if they could build on the small hope Brooke had handed him today, right now was not the time to surprise her with his appearance. Emotions were running too high from the fright of Brooke's kidnapping.

Leaning forward, he pressed a kiss to his cousin's forehead. "Where I live is a conversation for the grown-ups, but I'll keep you posted."

She grabbed him in a brief hug before she released him. He was halfway out the door when she spoke. "I love you, coz."

Ian didn't turn. She might see the tears standing in his eyes. Tears of relief. Acceptance. Hope. "Love you, too, kid."

Outside Meadow's room, he paused to let his emotions settle. So much was happening so fast. He was feeling for the first time.

Love for his family. Love from God.

Love for the woman on the other side of that door.

The kind of love he'd never imagined would flow to him or through him.

He patted his jeans pocket, tapped lightly on the half-open door, then stepped inside.

Meadow was standing by the window, looking out at the world. "I'm so ready to get home. I haven't been away from Grace this long…ever." She turned, eyebrow arched in question. "How did it go with Brooke? She's a great kid."

Suddenly, he didn't want to talk about anything but them. Their future. With three long strides, he walked around the end of her hospital bed, wrapped his arms around her and kissed her the way he'd promised to the day before. The way he'd wanted to before he'd even *realized* he wanted to.

And she met him with all of the emotion he was feeling, leaning into him in a way that let him support her yet also held him up. The way it had always been between them.

The way it should be.

He had no doubt when he pulled the ring from his pocket she'd say yes. No doubt they would share a life together that was somehow both exciting and settled.

He was ready to come out of the darkness and the woods. Ready to love and be loved.

Now and forever.

* * * * *

If you enjoyed this story, don't miss Trail of Threats, *the next book in the Mountain Country K-9 Unit series!*

Baby Protection Mission
by Laura Scott, April 2024

Her Duty Bound Defender
by Sharee Stover, May 2024

Chasing Justice
by Valerie Hansen, June 2024

Crime Scene Secrets
by Maggie K. Black, July 2024

Montana Abduction Rescue
by Jodie Bailey, August 2024

Trail of Threats
by Jessica R. Patch, September 2024

Tracing a Killer
by Sharon Dunn, October 2024

Search and Detect
by Terri Reed, November 2024

Christmas K-9 Guardians
by Lenora Worth and Katy Lee, December 2024

Available only from Love Inspired Suspense.

Discover more at LoveInspired.com.

Dear Reader,

How much fun is this Mountain Country K-9 Unit series? We've all had a blast chatting through the storyline and getting to know our characters. I'm honored to be working alongside some of my favorite writers to bring these characters to life. And these K-9s! I just love them!

I won't lie though, y'all. Ian was a tough one to figure out. He was very good at hiding his hurts, even from me. It wasn't until he saw his aunt face-to-face that his heart started to show. Let's be real, life throws us curveballs. It hurts. And some of our worst hurts come from the people closest to us.

Family pain is a tough pain to walk through. It's the cutting kind. Several years ago, God reminded me that He is the one who placed me in my family, in all of the beautiful and in all of the painful. He knew every single moment of my life before it happened. I love the image of Psalm 139, where it says He wrote down every day of my life in a book before I was ever born. (How could a writer not love that?) There's so much peace in knowing that He already knows what's coming and has made a plan for it. I may not always see that plan or understand it, but it's there. For me, there's no greater comfort in this life. God knows. God cares. I pray that, no matter what you're walking through, you can rest in the fact that He's already charted a path through it.

Until next time, drop by jodiebailey.com if you want to sign up for the newsletter or just say hi. And enjoy the rest of the books in the Mountain Country K-9 Unit series!

Jodie Bailey